The Legacy Solution

Ron Couch

PublishAmerica
Baltimore

First printing

ISBN: 1-60441-966-0
PUBLISHED BY PUBLISHAMERICA, LLLP
www.publishamerica.com
Baltimore

Printed in the United States of America

Sheldon Clark—CEO of Mega Motors Corporation
Kurt Schmidt—MM Chief of Security
Heinrich Schmidt—Kurt's Father
Elsie Schmidt—Kurt's Mother
David Wentz—Mossad Operative
Ryan Conway—MM Benefit Representative
Red O'Brien—MM Production Supervisor
Eleanor Brewer—Sheldon Clark's Secretary
J.D. Loving—MM Building Janitor/UAW District Committeeman
Earl Baker—MM Production Supervisor
Max Griebel—Clark's Gardener
Liz Lange—Schmidt's Secretary
Holly—Owner—Holly's Dating Service
Monique—Employee of Holly's Dating Service
Calviston "Crutch Tip" Jamison—MM Building Janitor/Composer/Singer
Hans Burger—SSS Reich Fuhrer

One

Placidly, suited directors exited the plush, blue-carpeted, soundproofed conference room on the fourteenth floor of the MM building located on Woodward Avenue in Detroit, Michigan.

Their steps were short—nearly duck-like. Many wore brown tasseled loafers—others, traditional black wing tips. Several scuffed their soles and heels across the nylon carpet creating considerable static electricity in an already charged atmosphere. There were no non-conservatively dressed individuals among them.

The magnificent structure, designed by renowned architect Albert Kahn in the 1920s, was, at the time, the nation's largest office building, consisting of four twelve-story wings and two additional stories for senior executives. Construction was completed in 1923. Elevators rose to the twelfth floor, and special lifts transported the elite to the fourteenth floor.

In 1996, MM purchased the Rialto Tower on the Detroit River and began moving their offices from the old headquarters on Woodward Avenue. The Rialto looked like a huge windowed tin can. It was undoubtedly the most unique building in downtown Detroit.

A security staff of twelve, some former police officers, FBI and CIA agents, encircled the chief executive and briskly ushered the CEO toward his office.

Mr. Sheldon Eugene Clark was small in stature, a little narrow-shouldered man. The beefy guards surrounding Mr. Clark towered above him. As they approached his sturdy oak office door, the circle of protection opened, allowing entrance for the extremely unpopular Chairman and CEO of Mega Motors Corporation.

Once inside, doors closed and locked, Clark walked into his private bath, splashed cool water on his blotchy cheeks and freckled forehead, dried, and allowed himself a glance into his beveled bathroom mirror. His reflection revealed a tad of smugness, arrogance and superiority. The corners of his mouth tilted up slightly and his thin lips separated just enough to expose small, flat yellow teeth. He had acquired a disgustingly bad habit of quickly darting his tongue in and out of the left corner of his mouth when he was in middle school. He tongue-darted quite often and, to critical observers, resembled a monitor lizard. Clark did not realize he had this tongue-darting affliction. He then walked behind his massive mahogany desk and slowly sank into an overstuffed imported black leather executive chair that subtly whooshed as his five-foot-five-inch one-hundred-forty-five-pound body relaxed. His tongue flicked and darted.

It was four fourteen P.M. The meeting had gone extraordinarily well. Clark assured his underlings the ten-year plan had commenced as scheduled. Bonuses would be doubled, perhaps tripled. All had contributed to the plan, and were sworn to secrecy as to the sweeping changes that had and would continue to drastically affect every individual that worked for or had any economic relationship with the corporation. Top executives, of course, would be exempted. Written memos with any reference to the plan had been specifically forbidden. The methods employed were personally inputted by the executives with top priority clearance on a secure network of computers. After all the plans were implemented, hard drives would be destroyed.

The plan was simple, yet vicious with no regard to human suffering. Clark and his selected executives were businesspersons of course. They were not social workers or care givers. Their job was to make a profit for the corporation. Out of profit came bonuses and stock options, preferred stock, preference stock and power—real power.

The hierarchy at MM was akin to a caste system. The upper echelon of the organization was exceedingly well compensated. These shooters were megalomaniacs to a man, and a few token females. They were the Jeffrey Dahmers of the business world, but viewed themselves as saviors of the automotive industry. They felt omnipotent.

MM's caste system created such insulated layers of management that few knew what was really going on. The big shots truly did not have a clue what was happening in the manufacturing and assembly plants, sales and engineering sections. They cared only about money, power and control. They were heartless. MM's Detroit headquarters was a hen house filled with roosters. The higher the office, the higher the position, and the more difficult it became to see folks on the streets below. From the top floors, people below resembled ants—and that was exactly how they were to be treated. They were ordinary, useless and common—things to be crushed.

Two

The first national agreement between the United Auto Workers and Mega Motors Corporation occurred in September of 1938. It was a historical agreement between the corporation and the UAW-CIO.

Now, as then, MM views the agreements as impediments, and of no real consequence. After all, the corporation still had the right to hire and fire at will. Some UAW executives were on the take. The seemingly never-ending battle between management and the union was a myth, perpetuated on a local plant basis only fodder for the media. Many of the union leaders at the international headquarters knew the "fighting" was a fraud. Capitalism flourished among both union and management executives. Circumstances were directly opposite those envisioned by founders of MM and the union.

Clark, of course, knew how it would all play out. The plan was fail safe. He had conceived it years before his graduation from the Mega Motors Institute in Lansing, Michigan. He merely waited until he ascended to the position of top dog at MM before it could be put into effect. The most threatening and challenging facet of Clark's plan was the selection of men and women in whom he could put his trust. Money, lots of it, could buy loyalty, trust and conscience. It was indeed rare to find a man or woman who would not or did not succumb to the allure of fame, fortune, and power. Those rarities were discharged. They were not team players. They could not be on Clark's squad.

Clark lived in a gated mansion in West Bloomfield, Michigan, with his wife of twenty-seven years, Phyllis. They had two children, Seth, twenty-five, and Beth, twenty-three. Both were married and living in California. They seldom called, unless they needed money or had a desire to extol the many virtues of California living. Beth appeared at Christmas, and Seth in July. They were rotten, spoiled rich kids. Phyllis was involved in community activities, bridge clubs, and church affairs. She volunteered her services as "book lady" at William Beaumont Hospital in Royal Oak. She could care less about Clark, but appreciated the no spending limit on her credit cards. Clark recognized the value of her lack of interest in his job. He neither knew nor cared to know his neighbors. He seldom saw them as he rarely went outside, other than to his office in Detroit. His pale skin burned easily. Had his neighbors known him, they would have disliked Clark immensely.

Their manicured weed-free Marion bluegrass lawn and flowerbeds were meticulously maintained by a full-time gardener who had worked for Sheldon's father, a retired MM executive accountant. Clark hated the old German gardener, but out of deference to his deceased father, kept the old man employed. Max smelled like a goat and despised Clark. He recognized him for the wimp he was. Max had no CEO—no ladder to climb. The lawn was watered with an automatic sprinkling system. Max Griebel was a quiet, cantankerous, old man, but a darn good gardener. He often wondered how Mr. Clark Sr. could have sired his current employer.

Clark attended a huge local Presbyterian church, Kirk of the Hills, with his wife, Phyllis. He did not tithe. He merely passed the donation plate along. He never joined in with the singing of hymns. He thought the minister was a doltish clod. His primary reason for attending church was status related. He was not an atheist, agnostic, or Gnostic. He was not a deist. If asked, however, he was a Christian. It was politically correct to be a Christian. Clark's true deity was power.

Of all the members of Clark's security staff, he had one favorite. Kurt Schmidt and Clark met in high school. They were not friends in the true sense of the word, but formed a bond of resentment against any person or group of people with sheep-like mentality; virtually everyone not as intelligent as Clark and Schmidt perceived themselves. Clark vowed he would someday change the status-quo at MM, and eliminate the herd of lemmings that were slowly sinking the corporation into a giant lake of crimson ink. There were enough great lakes surrounding Michigan, Clark thought.

After Clark's meteoric rise to power at MM, he discovered his high school acquaintance, Kurt Schmidt, had been a Detroit police officer, and subsequently promoted to the rank of a detective. The two met at the Roma Café in Detroit's Eastern market, and within a short period, Kurt was working for Clark as his security chief. Schmidt did not know, but assumed he was thoroughly investigated before the job offer was made. Clark became aware Kurt had been a no-nonsense patrol officer who had killed no fewer than three felons in the line of duty. The killings were deemed justifiable by a Detroit police investigative court of review. Kurt knew it was highly unlikely anyone would ever find the other weighted bodies, some having rotted away, other torsos listing eerily in the sixteen miles per hour current on the black silt bottom of the cold murky waters of the Detroit River.

Kurt Schmidt, like Sheldon Clark, refused to take vacation time off, and both reported to work on holidays and weekends, often as early as six A.M. Were they workaholic? Undoubtedly. It was Thanksgiving when Clark finally confided to Kurt Schmidt the true, violent, but absolutely necessary nature of the plan. Had Schmidt been opposed to the strategy, he would have been summarily discharged, but Clark knew his man. Both were visionaries.

"Kurt, what I'm going to tell you may sound intense, but it is in the best interest of the corporation." Clark looked closely for any response from Kurt.

There was none. The only physical reaction noticeable to Clark was the widening of Schmidt's nostrils—and that barely perceptible.

Schmidt, however, noticed Clark's tongue flicking and darting in and out of the left corner of his mouth. He had to force himself to look elsewhere as an inner rage started to develop, and he could ill afford to lose his composure at this time.

Clark continued. "You know, MM continues to downsize and out source. Much progress has been made in reducing the number of salaried and hourly employees. The North American UAW active membership has declined from 1,600,000 to a current level of approximately 69,000. The salaried work force is fewer than 30,000, down from 150,000, and still shrinking. There are more than 400,000 retirees and the number is constantly growing. It appears we cannot get rid of people quickly enough. They do not die soon enough. We continue to reduce medical benefits. Cost of living allowance, once payable to salaried employees, was eliminated. Thousands of salaried people have retired under the special early retirement provisions. The stupid fools actually believed we would continue to provide medical benefits at no cost to them. It continues to give me a personal thrill when these serfs, knaves, and fools, who thought of themselves as leaders, and part of the Team, finally realize they are not, and were never important—not in the least.

"Kurt, I owe the stockholders more than merely the downsizing of the company and increasing share value. Any idiot can shrink a company. My goal is to diminish legacy costs. I will not rest until we have complete control over legacy costs. I mean complete and total. Are you with me?"

Showing hungry anticipation in his clear light-blue eyes, Kurt said, "Of course I'm with you. I've been meaning to tell you. This job of security chief is very boring. When does the new assignment begin?"

Clark smiled the grin of an opossum eating feces. Kurt remained stolid, void of emotion. Both men shook hands sealing the agreement. Clark replied, "The sooner, the better. Remember, no holds barred." Clark cackled a disgusting childish giggle, and tongue-darted rapidly. Schmidt again became incensed, but still managed to remain outwardly emotionless and cool.

Three

Ryan Conway pressed the start button that activated one of two huge electric drive motors that in turn drove the variable speed assembly line at ninety units per hour. The line consisted of fifty-two, T-shaped assembly fixtures, each bolted to a steel plate—the steel plate attached to a chain-link metal belt that smoothly traveled a distance of fifty yards. The assembled units were transported to a shipping dock on plastic-coated steel hooks, specially designed for this product, by way of an overhead monorail conveyor. The assemblies were unloaded and placed in shipping racks, and the filled racks transported to railroad cars, and shipped to various MM final assembly plants. The empty fixtures then turned 180 degrees on a huge sprocket en route to their underground trip back to the beginning of the operation. The process, designed in Germany, was quite modern for the time.

It was exactly seven A.M. and all thirty assemblers were in place, ready to begin work as the signal sounded. Well, most of the assemblers were ready. In reality, every morning, two or three folks were late and one or two were absent. The relief men went into action and substituted until Ryan could beg, borrow or steal workers from other departments that could afford to lend them out for the day. The first fifteen to twenty minutes of every day was nerve-wracking. There was no excuse for shutting the assembly line down during working hours—none whatsoever.

The product was the MM front cross members' assembly. It consisted of a cross member, two lower control arms, two upper control arms, two coil springs, two dust shields, two steering knuckles, four greased bearings, two grease seals and four ball joints. Two brake caliper assemblies, two rotors, two tie rod ends, a steering rod, and a handful of nuts, bolts and lock washers, cotter pins and a couple of hub caps and you had a cross member assembly. It seemed complex, but was the very opposite. Simplicity was a necessary component of any efficient assembly line.

Ryan Conway, although a relatively young man, was a father figure for most of his employees. Most would confide to Ryan of their most personal problems and secrets. One of his relief men once told him he had special feelings for young white boys. He knew more than he cared to know about their families, divorces, drinking habits and health problems. He seldom confided his own issues to his employees, thinking it totally inappropriate. Ryan was slightly above average height and weighed 180 pounds. His once thick light brown hair had thinned, especially on the crown of his head. He was able to cover the spot fairly well with innovative combing, but feared it would eventually be bald.

One afternoon after work, several of his employees invited Ryan to attend and participate in a softball game at a ball diamond located at Freedom Hill in Detroit. Ryan happily accepted the invitation and joined not only the game, playing the position of left field, but also in the liquid refreshments.

After seven innings, Ryan and eight of his crew drove to an east side, a topless bar where they continued drinking until two A.M. The topless dancers were not among Detroit's finest. They exhibited stretch marks, appendix scars and lumps of cellulite, but they tried to be entertaining. By last call, some actually looked quite fetching—lumpy cellulite and all.

At the start of the next morning's shift, five of Ryan's key people were late reporting to work. They were wild eyed and nervous, but laughed nervously at their foolishness of the previous night. One of the missing key people was Ryan, who was twenty-two minutes late.

Ryan's general supervisor, Anton Washington, was attempting to start operations, but did not have the foggiest notion how to coordinate activities. There were more assembly fixtures running empty than not. Anton was so relieved when he saw Ryan, he forgot about being angry realizing Ryan and his crew would soon have things in working order. Within minutes, Anton returned to his office and began working on a crossword puzzle—one he never solved without help from Ryan.

The other four tardy employees gradually reported to work. After such a shoddy start—losing nearly thirty-six units—it appeared to be the beginning of a very inefficient day, but, urged on by the majority of the employees, Ryan increased the line speed to ninety-five units per hour, and at the end of the day, the total production was seven-hundred and twenty. The line again ran efficiently, and everyone was happy—including Anton.

Anton and Ryan developed a friendship not often seen between supervisors and general supervisors. It made little difference to either that one of them was not Caucasian. One evening Ryan drove to Anton's house in Detroit where he was introduced to Anton's wife and kids. The kids stared at Ryan as though he were odd. Ryan and Anton left in Ryan's 1976 Corvette and frequented several neighborhood bars and had a great time. The next time Ryan went to Anton's house, he discovered they were in the midst of a divorce. It was very sad, as they appeared to be a great little family.

Anton felt strongly his race had been and was still discriminated against, and Ryan agreed wholeheartedly. Where they differed was the means by which past and present racism could be addressed and corrected. Both realized it would not happen overnight. Ryan felt that because his ancestors had been too poor to own slaves, he and his relatives should not be involved in any retribution. Anton firmly believed Blacks should be granted certain opportunities before Whites—employment, educational, etc., to help atone for the sins of racism, regardless whether or not one's relatives owned a slave. The two never agreed on that issue but remained friends, which, Ryan thought, was a positive sign that the matter of racism and discrimination was slowly resolving itself.

The group of young assemblers was mostly twenty to thirty years of age. Men, women, black and white, a couple of Mexicans, an Arab, a former beauty queen, an American Indian, and others from assorted backgrounds made for a very diverse department. Most were high school graduates. One was a college graduate. One was an ex-con who had spent a few years in Jackson State prison. She was a vicious arrogant woman, considered a "Protected" employee by the Personnel Department; that is protected from discipline or discharge by her direct supervisor. She and a few dozen others throughout the plant were "hard core" employees—former occupants of Michigan jails and prisons paroled by the weakened judicial systems and hired by MM and other auto companies in an idiotic stunt to impress the liberal politicians and gullible public as to how wonderful and caring the car companies were.

The "hard-core" employees was a small, but violent component of the three shift operations of nearly three thousand five hundred employees. Their assignments were typical mundane repetitive jobs—not too easy—not too hard—all very boring and tedious. Many a night's sleep was interrupted worrying about hard-core employees. It was analogous to training a mad dog or alligator. It simply could not be done.

Of the approximate fifty "hard-cores," notwithstanding the fact free transportation and lunches were made available until these people got their first paycheck, five quit on their first day of employment. Five more did not return to work the second day, and twelve disappeared after their first paycheck. Of the remaining twenty-eight, eighteen were AWOL in two weeks. Of the remaining ten, one overdosed and died, and two filed workers' compensation claims for alleged back injuries.

One of the claimants was nicknamed butt-hole buster while in Jackson State prison serving a stint for armed robbery, and the other had converted to Islam while incarcerated for rape, armed robbery and kidnapping.

The convert had changed his name to Ahmad. The buster went on sick leave and then filed a worker's compensation claim for back injuries. Buster's day in court netted him five hundred dollars. When he signed his redemption papers, MM was rid of him for good. The lawyers representing MM had authorization to redeem the case up to five thousand dollars.

Ahmad was more complicated. His workers' compensation case was for aggravation of a back injury, which occurred initially in Jackson State prison in a slip-fall incident in one of the prison showers. MM was ordered to pay Ahmad weekly compensation benefits, medical bills, and back pay by a liberal Michigan Bureau of Workers' Disability Compensation administrative law judge.

Surprisingly, Ahmad returned to work at MM-Warren in less than one month and expressed his desire to become a supervisor to Ryan, after Ryan had been transferred to the Personnel Department.

Ryan's thoughts floated somewhere between laughter and anger after hearing Ahmad's verbal plea of wanting to improve his lot in life, so he told Ahmad he would see that the proper people in personnel would be made aware of his ambitions.

Within a month, Ahmad was back out on sick leave. His back just gave out. He returned to the trough to join thousands of others who would rather take than give.

The hard core employees resented authority—white authority, black authority, male or female. They seemed to despise ties, white shirts, dress shirts and any uniform that represented a figure of dominance. The hatred could be sensed and seen in their eyes and mannerisms. One African American female hard core cold-cocked an African American supervisor so hard he nearly lost consciousness, yet he was forbidden to discharge this person. The supervisor, Jim Hughes, made the mistake of asking Tamika Johnson why she had been late reporting to work. She responded with a vicious right hook, flooring Hughes in front of several mortified employees, and would have done severe bodily damage had some nearby co-workers not restrained her. She went hog-wild. Ultimately, she was terminated for failure to report to work.

Ryan was forty years old, having spent fifteen years on the plant floor as an inspection supervisor, and for the last six years as a production supervisor. He knew his chances for promotion to general supervisor had been dashed years prior after calling a production superintendent an ignorant moron at the annual MM-Warren golf outing. Ryan's tongue got too loose after he drank too much, and he drank too much too often. He had been told after one particular mouthing-off incident his chances for advancement were slim to none. He continued to harbor some hope of advancement, but as the years slowly passed by, his hope diminished. Ryan had been his own worst enemy. He was unable to cope with the surreal life of managing the unmanageable.

Ryan discovered he could not handle the nonstop pressure exerted by seemingly everyone in charge, and abhorred the daily whining of at least two or three employees. He found it intensely boring and time consuming, but Ryan had to appear interested. The constant struggle to attain and maintain efficiency, quality, safety, and morale was relentless. These same goals had to be impressed upon each one of Ryan's employees to assure compliance with all requirements. The younger employees, at least a high percentage of them, frankly could care less about efficiency, quality and morale. They seemed to have been born with a something for nothing attitude, and were not about to change to please Ryan or their fellow employees. So, production supervisors like Ryan and Red simply did the best they could, knowing, in higher management's eyes, it would never be good enough. It was a sad and thankless, sorry situation.

Ryan's job setter, Rob Sizemore, was a Godsend. Rob all but ran the assembly line and the adjacent feeder department that assembled black painted control arm subassemblies for the main line. Rob was smart, dedicated, and a terrific mechanic. He was smooth with women both off and on the job. One morning, Ryan needed Rob's assistance on a torque problem, but could not find him. He asked one of the relief men if he had seen Rob, and the employee pointed to a large black shipping container. Ryan walked to the container, peeked over the five-foot door and saw Rob and Laverne, a tall, slender black lady assembler, having wild, screaming, animal sex. Obviously, it was in violation of one of the forty-three shop rules, but Ryan could not remember which one, and decided to pretend he did not see the action.

In-plant sex was not uncommon. What was odd was discovering those in the act. There were many hiding places in the factory, especially on the second and third shifts, when many of the bright mercury vapor lights were shut off in areas that operated on the day shift only.

One night on the third shift, Ryan, who was walking through building four, observed a man standing watch in the aisle adjacent to the old truck front steering knuckle job. The lookout let out a loud yelp that disengaged two young males giving and receiving anal sex. Although Ryan could have, and should have penalized all three, he chose to ignore the infraction and simply walked away shaking his head in disgust.

Ryan Conway could perform all the jobs on the assembly line. All but the spring compression job that he, frankly, had no interest in doing after seeing one of his assemblers get hit square in the gonads after improperly positioning the coil spring in the compression fixture. The spring flew out, hit the steel conveyor and bounced angrily into Bob Dombrowski's crotch. Bob clutched himself, screamed, and fell to the shop floor. Rob, who was nearby, helped Bob to his feet and assumed the spring compression job insuring the line would continue to run, and not skip a beat. Bob was bruised and embarrassed, but not seriously injured. He resumed his normal activity within five minutes of groaning and shame.

This assembly line itself was more complex than one might imagine. A tremendous amount of interaction with other departments was necessary in order for it to run at all. The material department furnished the assemblers with parts—nuts, bolts, washers, and dozens of other components. The parts were delivered by battery powered hi lows. One driver, Homer the Hat, was generally drunk, but still got the job done. General Lee was sober, but moody as the blues. The Baker hi low weighs 14,000 to 16,000 pounds, discounting the gross and tare weight of the containers and parts contained therein.

A group of skilled tradesmen stationed nearby and serviced the line in the event of mechanical, pneumatic, hydraulic or electrical failure. Dozens of compressed air lines operated dozens of air guns, each calibrated to achieve required torque on their designated function. This group of journeymen consisted of electricians, pipe fitters, millwrights, tinsmiths, machine repairmen, and tool and die makers. Several of the tool and die makers were born in Germany. One had actually worked in a Messerschmitt factory and felt Germany should have won WWII. Many of the maintenance employees were from the south—good old boys.

Additionally, several inspectors were assigned to the line to insure quality of the product, made a daily accounting of scrap, taking torque checks on nuts and bolts, performed visual inspections and other quality checks. Several inspectors had worked for Ryan when he was an inspection supervisor, and their working relationship was excellent. They knew Ryan would not intentionally allow defective material to be shipped to assembly plants.

There was also a janitor assigned to the line who provided normal janitorial services such as sweeping, emptying trashcans and other miscellaneous cleaning functions. He was a huge man, around six foot five and weighed in at 260 pounds. His nickname was Animal. The Animal was an Elvis look alike in a perverted sort of way. He had dark greasy straight hair, long arms, and a big belly. He was also very much an alcoholic, consuming on average two fifths of Mohawk vodka per day. The Animal also imbibed Popov vodka when Mohawk was not available. Ryan figured Animal might even drink mouthwash should liquor stores ever run out of Mohawk and Popov. His physician had told animal repeatedly that if he continued to drink alcohol, he would die. It was sad to see Animal slowly but surely drink himself to death.

Ryan attended Animal's funeral and was the only salaried employee having the decency to show his respect to the Animal. Many union brothers and sisters visited the funeral home, but no close friends or relatives showed up. Apparently, he had no living relatives or close friends. Such are the life and death of many alcoholics. Ryan thought, it's no the wonder union employee held management in such disdain and contempt. Somewhere along the way, management and the union had forgotten to respect each another.

MM had an unwritten policy about supervisors hanging out with their employees and assumed a relationship between a worker and his boss could affect the supervisor's ability to perform his job. In short, higher management held low-level supervision in disdain. If one's ability to choose friends was questioned, then one should equally question those making those judgments. Ryan had more respect for his employees than he had for higher supervision and was harshly criticized for his selection of friends. Ryan could have cared less. His pals in the union were generally not two-faced like many in management.

The employees who reported to him respected Ryan. He was their boss and friend. To a man (and a woman) they knew Ryan would be a tough disciplinarian, if necessary. More important, they knew he was fair. Ryan had learned that mutual respect was necessary to attain maximum performance from any person or group of individuals.

Occasionally, openings would occur for promotion within the department's hourly ranks. As production requirement increased, more workers were required, and openings for the classification of four relief persons, a job paying a few cents more per hour, were available.

Ryan had his favorites, but he selected individuals strictly according to their seniority. Even though this process was, contractually, the appropriate thing to do, it had been largely ignored by supervisors in the past, and those upgraded were generally the favorites and pals and brown-noses of the supervisor and general supervisor.

Although an upgrade to the classification of a relief person paid just pennies more per hour, it was an opportunity to escape the monotony of repetitious boredom, and those asked to accept the upgrade were extremely grateful. Surprisingly, the line's one and only college graduate, Cass Madurski, declined the opportunity for promotion stating he was happy doing his current job of assembly and was not interested in doing anything else. Ryan could do no more than ask and encourage.

While higher management attempted to insist safety and housekeeping were the main priorities at all MM US manufacturing and assembly locations, essentially volume of parts out the door was the name of the game. Next to quantity came quality and efficiency of operation. Each job, whether in the manufacturing, assembly of components or assembly of vehicles was time studied by standard's departments with stop watches and an actual time frame was given to every time factor involved in the manufacturing of parts, subassemblies, assemblies, stamping and machining operations, and so forth.

In short, a standard time is assigned a particular product, i.e., the standard time times the number of items produced equals standard hours. Should the standard hours exceed actual man hours expended to produce a certain number of units, it was a simple matter of multiplication and division to convert the hours into a percentage of efficiency for the day's run. Conversely, should man hours required exceed standard hours acquired in a production run, it was then calculated the department had run inefficiently, and there was never an acceptable reason for running an operation inefficiently. It was standard procedure for the supervisor to be summoned to the production superintendent's office, after working hours, and be grilled unmercifully as to his unsatisfactory performance.

Ryan could think of nothing more humiliating and degrading than to be chewed out after having worked so hard—having done his absolute best, along with the men and women in his department—only to be grilled on poor performance. Therefore, he stood there and took it, as all supervisors did.

Four

Kurt entered his SUV parked in the MM company car garage at 9:05 P.M. Friday evening. The company-owned vehicle was fully fueled, washed and vacuumed. Having driven his vehicle nearly six months, he would soon be furnished another SUV or any MM vehicle he chose. He buckled up and slowly drove the big 4x4 out of the garage and within minutes merged onto northbound I-75 to the suburbs where he would find his modest two-thousand-square-foot colonial in Sterling Heights. Only one idiot cut him off on his way home. Kurt hoped the driver who narrowly missed clipping the front bumper of his SUV would die a horrible death. He envisioned the discourteous driver colliding with a gasoline tanker and burning to death in the terrible catastrophic ensuing explosion. These thoughts calmed Kurt Schmidt.

Kurt lived alone, having never married. When his carnal desires flamed, he simply called a dating service, and within minutes, whomever he desired would be chauffeured to his home, and returned via the same limousine. He insisted on complete and utter secrecy concerning his sex life, and made it perfectly clear to the madam, known as Whorehouse Holly, he would have no compunction whatsoever to butcher her and her two fatherless children should anyone ever be made aware of his sexual proclivities. Kurt gave considerable thought to eliminating her and her kids regardless. These thoughts gave him incredibly wondrous pleasure.

At 9:47 P.M., Kurt was home, sitting on his favorite recliner, drinking the first of many Grolsch Lager beers. Friday was the only day he allowed himself to overindulge. Tomorrow, he would start assembling the task force necessary to address the issue at hand—legacy costs. He chuckled a mean man's chuckles and involuntarily salivated imagining the taste and smell of blood and carnage.

One of life's true pleasure for Kurt Schmidt was inflicting pain on others. He had been a brutal bully as long as he could remember. He was a big man at six four and two hundred thirty-one pounds and had no preference to whom he caused pain and discomfort. He grew in the suburbs of Van Dyke, Michigan, just north of Detroit and attended Van Dyke public schools. He made no particular academic achievement, but was a good, aggressive linebacker on the high school football team.

After graduating from high school, Kurt joined the Marines where he became more keenly aware of his ability to inflict great bodily harm on others. He also trained as a demolition expert assigned to an explosive ordinance team. After his enlistment ended in the Corps, Corporal Schmidt donned civilian clothes, moved to Detroit to establish residency and eventually became a police officer with the Detroit Police Department. He found the required training simple and boring compared to the rigid physical and mental discipline required by the Marines.

Initially, Kurt could not get enough action as a Detroit cop, even though he and his partner, a seasoned officer of seven years, were constantly being dispatched to a myriad of people problems—some criminal—some domestic in nature. He enjoyed viewing the blood, guts, and gore seen so often in the streets and homes of Detroit's drug-addicted, murderous neighborhoods.

Kurt spent many of his off hours assuming the role of manic plain clothes' cop, even though he was still a police officer—a rookie. He frequented sleazy bars where dopers and perverts hung out. He became familiar with pimps, hookers, and the ilk of the east side of Detroit. For a few weeks, he simply observed, but finally decided to become proactive.

He was quite intelligent and aggressive and promoted to the position of detective. He missed the hands-on action almost immediately.

Schmidt soon tired of protecting, serving and completing endless forms of ridiculous paperwork. In his view, whatever force necessary should eliminate criminals. A criminal was anyone who broke the law or who simply angered him. Kurt Schmidt's ambitious destiny was to eliminate, to kill, to maim, and destroy. Therefore, he did.

Kurt's father, Heinrich Schmidt, was a decorated officer in Hitler's elite SS, one of Germany's most brutal, efficient, and heartless weapons of torture and death. Hitler's security staff was extremely loyal to the fuhrer and believed, to a man, in their superiority as Aryans. Before he fled faltering Germany, near the end of World War II, Heinrich and Kurt, who was then eleven years old, left Berlin. Heinrich had previously directed that his wife, Elsie, to be butchered along with Kurt's German shepherd, Pupa, in a show of faith and humility to the fuhrer and Germany. Kurt adored his father.

How the father and son Schmidt managed to enter the United States undetected is unknown. Heinrich and Kurt moved to Detroit, Michigan, where the elder Schmidt obtained employment at Hudson Motor Car Company as an electrician, a skill he acquired in Germany before the war. Heinrich Schmidt was an excellent electrician and employee. He had a nearly perfect attendance record and appeared to be a quiet, humble man. One would never have suspected his having been a former SS officer.

Heinrich was killed in an industrial accident several years later and Kurt moved from Detroit to a wealthy uncle's home in Grosse Pointe, MI, an upscale suburb of Detroit, located in northeast Wayne County near Lake Saint Claire. Grosse Point Park, Woods, and Farms constitute the communities of the city of Grosse Pointe.

Once a haven for many extremely affluent automobile executives, but for the past several years, most of these millionaires moved further away from the shores to establish residence in West Bloomfield Hills in Oakland County and other ritzy areas north of the Motor City.

Many of the white middle class residents of Detroit, having moved north for employment from Appalachia, moved out of Detroit when they became financially able to do so. The moves were not racially motivated, but simply a cycle noted in the majority of major cities. The move to suburbia was a goal of many—from the large city to a smaller community—a dream fulfilled.

Five

Sheldon Clark, Chairman and CEO of MM Corporation, had always looked like a wimp. His stature was small, complexion pale, with freckles and acne scars. His thin dishwater blond hair looked dry and unhealthy. His puny physical appearance plus an effeminate voice and an ever-present body odor and foul breath made him very difficult to like. Sheldon had no heart, compassion or conscience. His hands were small, almost effeminate. He loathed people. He was an ideal executive.

Clark was an absolute genius with numbers. While an engineering student at the University of Michigan, he loved and excelled in statistics and other courses of challenging curriculums. His goal was to strengthen the existing MM caste system ruthlessly eliminating whatever or whomever he perceived as unnecessary. He was a bean counter at heart, and a prickish wimp.

Clark led through fear and oppression, not out of respect or by example. Those who objected to his methods were swiftly transferred to MM plants in Buffalo or Tonawanda, NY, or Saginaw forge, in Saginaw, MI, for "training." He methodically excised individuals he felt would be a threat to his solution. Actually, he directed others to do the dirty work. He hated face-to-face confrontation. He insisted on having armed guards at his beck and call.

Clark's's wife, Phyliss, held him in contempt, but never expressed those views. He was, after all, a good provider. They slept in separate bedrooms in their West Bloomfield five-thousand-square-foot mansion. Clark suspected Phyliss was a wanna-be lesbian. She was an ordinary-looking woman, even with the help of make-up. The kids were gone. Money was abundant. Clark's idea of a good time was having a dream about out sourcing, and occasionally about down sourcing his wife. Life was good. He was insulated against hearing anyone making demeaning statements about him. He was a powerful man.

He loathed the spotlight the position of authority had placed him in. When possible, Clark delegated his media appearances to his subordinates. Clark felt he was above having to explain his actions to anyone. He hated interacting with people. He sometimes wished he had been born good looking, but felt attractive men were ignorant. He settled for being intelligent, and ruthless.

During obligatory meetings with his executive staff, and top shareholders, he read scripted statements, previously proofed by the MM legal staff. He took no questions. His statements were boring and bland. Very few attendees were interested in anything he read and jumped at the opportunity to leave. Of course, the staff pretended to be transfixed by his statements. The role-playing was a facade, an integral part of being an executive. Clark hated role-play.

Much to Mr. Clark's dismay, the janitorial services of the executive offices, including his, were provided by hourly rated, UAW union members. They were classified, Janitor—office. He loathed the fact that a lowly peon custodian would walk into his office. He anticipated the day when this disgustingly low work could be outsourced to a non-union company.

Sheldon Clark's office janitor, J.D. Loving, was also a district committeeman, and disliked the arrogance of Mr. Clark as much as Mr. Clark disliked janitors. One Monday morning, before Mr. Clark arrived at work, J.D., who had finished cleaning Clark's bathroom, saw his toothbrush, and suddenly had an awakening. It took only seconds to remove the orange toothbrush from its holder, unzip his fly, drop his Levis to knee level, lower his boxer shorts, and comb his pubic hair with the orange toothbrush. The mental rush J.D. felt was nearly orgasmic. He checked the bristles closely for telltale pubic hair before putting Clark's toothbrush back in the holder.

At the next scheduled local union meeting, the brothers and sisters nearly fell out laughing after listening to J.D. Loving recall and recite, with great relish, and detail, the events of the toothbrush caper. J.D. became a living legend. He wore jeans to work. He owned an assortment of T-shirts with various logos ranging from MM logos to an airbrushed caricature of Alfred E. Neuman of *Mad Magazine* fame.

Six

MM-Warren was located on Eleven Mile Road in Warren, Michigan. Mega Motors acquired the property and buildings in the late 1950s for an insignificant amount of money. The facility had been previously used to produce ammunition for the US government by Ford Motor Company but had been abandoned and empty for more than seventeen years. Initially, there were fifteen separate buildings at the complex, but six or more were put under the same roof in a continuing effort to modernize the plant.

MM-Warren was a manufacturing facility and an offshoot of MM Gear and Axle in Livonia, Michigan. The first production jobs were the cross-shaft job, the wheel job, rear truck gear and axle assembly, front I-beam axle assembly, and miscellaneous stamping. United Auto Workers, Local 919, provided excellent representation for the hourly employee at MM-Warren. The Local had become a much-needed advocate of the Warren plant. While some of their leaders and members leaned hard left, overall the union, particularly Local 919, was sorely needed.

The plant grew in capacity and diversity from 1961 and remained a real asset for MM until sold to MM-Radiator division in 1982. The peak employment of MM-Warren reached around 3,800 in 1979. In 1965, there were eighteen MM final assembly plants in the United States.

The plant had a powerhouse, waste treatment facility, a complete metallurgical laboratory, and was in fact a city within a city complete with plant security patrolmen and officers—many ex military and police. There were a small fire engine and an adequate number of volunteer fire fighters comprising hourly and salary employees. There were underground tunnels going places only the rats knew, and these were giant factory rats, kept fat by slovenly employees, too lazy to properly dispose of their lunches.

The two-storied brick administration building housed the plant manager, purchasing, material, standards, master mechanics, accounting, and plant engineering personnel. The fanciest offices belonged to the plant manager and the resident comptroller. The plant manager had a complete photo album of all salary employees of the MM-Warren location. The album was built into a wall in his office on rotating shelves. The plant manager could view whomever he chose by pressing a remote control switch.

One particularly disgusting plant manager, Reginald Hammer, a drunken fellow, was so disliked by nearly everyone that late one evening several plant security officers decided they would kidnap an anteater from a nearby army base, place it in the plant manager's chair, and photograph it.

One of the security officers was a good friend of a Major stationed at the Mound Road army base. This same Major was the owner of a giant anteater, which he personally loathed, but kept caged behind his army-built house. He wanted to kill the wretched animal, but his twelve-year-old daughter adored the ugly thing. The predominantly gray animal had a black band bordered with white and was fully-grown, measuring four feet long, not including the two-foot-long tail.

The Major willingly let the security officer kidnap his anteater late one evening, provided it was returned before his daughter got up for school at seven the next morning.

The kidnapping was uneventful, although the normally docile animal did thrash about considerably in its cage. It took less than fifteen minutes to transport the hideous creature from the base to the plant manager's office. Four security officers volunteered for the transport assignment.

Soon, the animal, in all its hideous glory, was seated in Hammer's chair, behind his huge wooden desk. The camera, mounted on a tripod, was focused perfectly.

It was a gloriously wonderful plan until the anteater developed an instant bout of screaming diarrhea, squirting and spewing the most odorous and disgusting green excrement completely covering the chair, desk and carpeted floor. It took the security men the rest of the night to clean the foul mess and fumigate Hammer's office. They returned the wretched creature to the army base thirty-five minutes before the Major's daughter awoke.

An adjacent one-story brick building housed the personnel, hourly and salary, main medical facility, labor relations, safety and plant security staff. Dean Dugger, the personnel director, a smiling, car-salesperson type, had a very plush office and a foxy blond secretary named Eleanor. He also had the latest in recording devices concealed under his desk to record off-the-record conversations. He was a typical weasel-type personnel director.

Within the plant proper were two cafeterias (in better times, three)—open for breakfast, lunch and evening hours for the second shift employees. Each production building had several relief areas which had well-stocked banks of vending machines with hot and cold foods. Tables and chairs were provided for the employees. Smoking was allowed in the vast majority of the plant.

Locker rooms were made available for all employees, as were toilets and showers. There were also picnic areas outside the plant proper. Employee lockers held a vast array of items ranging from shoes and clothing to small kegs of beer, whisky, and an interesting assortment of illegal drugs.

Additionally, the plant employed a medical doctor and staff of nurses, EMT's, paramedics, as well as an ambulance that was dispatched in the event of an in-plant medical emergency. The doctors were trained in industrial medicine, whatever that entailed. As a rule, these physicians avoided private practice and people in general. Blood and gore situations were generally handled by the medical department's EMT's, paramedics and nurses, as the plant medical director was only there because he hated the field of medicine and could not survive as a real physician. There were few exceptions. A local ambulance company to nearby hospitals took injured employees requiring additional care. There was an occasional trauma so severe it resulted in subsequent death. These instances were rare. Dead employees were never pronounced dead on the scene.

There was an additional cafeteria between the administration and personnel buildings for salary and hourly employees as well as an executive dining room for the department heads, assistant department heads, general superintendents and the plant manager. The food prepared for the executives was top of the line. A vitamin was included with the executive meals. Food in the other cafeterias was edible, but many brought their own lunch from home. Some folks raced to nearby bars and drank their lunch. One enterprising pub actually provided transportation to and from their watering hole.

Theft from the south parking lot—the largest lot holding around fifteen-hundred vehicles continued to be an ongoing problem. Tires were stolen on a regular basis. Engines, transmissions, and, of course, entire vehicles were removed by a tireless, skilled gang of thieves.

Eventually, it was decided to secure all six large chain-link gates. They would be locked, excluding the starting and ending of the shifts, and lunchtime. This action did reduce theft, but hardly eliminated it. The criminals simply started stealing when the gates were open. One particularly imbecilic thief stole a Corvette and discovered the huge gates were closed. He decided to ram the west gate. He succeeded in destroying the beautiful yellow Corvette—incurring major injuries to his neck and head—plus a lengthy jail sentence.

The hourly employees also could avail themselves the use of a work out room equipped with the latest in body toning and exercise equipment, and was overseen by a physical therapist. This was a result of a fulfilled local union demand. Although many skeptics felt many injuries and claims for benefits would occur, this worry did not come to fruition.

Substance abuse personnel, both salary and hourly folks, were available to employees in need. At one time, salaried personnel provided MM insurance representatives on location to provide all necessary sickness and accident forms and issue payment to those on disability leaves of absence. Initially, very few alcoholics and drug addicts took advantage of the help offered by the substance abuse coordinator, but eventually, many did. It will never be known how many lives were saved or the number of family members who benefitted from the wise counsel of John Stafford, the plant's first and most effective substance abuse coordinator.

Other insurance needs were addressed also, such as medical, life, vision, hearing, life and dependent group insurance, hearing, pension administration and worker's disability compensation. There were many, many perks for the employees

Seven

Ryan had spent many years in the plant. He knew a little about every operation—a lot about others. He knew practically everyone in the plant, if not by name, by face. He could not walk one hundred feet without either acknowledging with a nod and smile or speaking to people with whom he had worked.

He had worked as either an inspection or a production supervisor in every area of the plant on every shift and had reported to a minimum of thirty-eight general supervisors—mostly good people. He knew and respected most of the union officials, realizing their job was not too much different from his. Actually, a committeeman's job could be much more stressful. On average, less than 3 percent of the employees were troublemakers as most employees who summoned their committeemen was just really bad news.

In the 1970s, MM decided it was past time to hire females and additional minorities. Prior to 1971, the racial mix at MM-Warren was around 85 percent white and 15 percent black—all males. Hundreds of blacks and females were hired and assigned randomly to all three major plant areas. It was bedlam.

The older seniority employee leered and lusted at the new female employees as though they had never seen a woman before. Even the crusty old supervisors tended to treat these ladies with kid gloves. Of course, this preferential treatment caused ill feelings among many employees, and that led to problems with morale. Soon, the newness wore off, and even though most of the females were given lighter jobs than men, all but the old-timers who would never be convinced women should work side by side near them eventually accepted them as co-workers. To them, females should be either home with the children or working as clerks and secretaries in the front offices.

Some of the women were easy prey for womanizers and sexual predators. One married lady had earned the reputation of having had sex with an entire department (approximately thirty men) one at a time, of course. Unfortunately, her husband and two of her sons worked at the same facility, and were painfully aware of her proclivity to breed. One of the plant pimps offered his managerial expertise to several females and some agreed to avail themselves of his contacts. Soon, the women were dually employed.

Other newly hired employees of the 1970s, at least a significant number of them, just flat did not want to work. They were lazy and not accustomed to boring, sometimes heavy repetitive tasks and resented any kind of authority. Ryan wondered, what are we supposed to do with this human garbage? Ryan and most other production, inspection and material department supervisors discharged at least 10 percent of newly hired as, "Unsatisfactory, temporary employees."

The foremen wondered and talked among themselves about the sorry state of the younger generation not realizing that as poor as these 1970s misfits were, new hires in future years would be worse—much worse. Ryan regretted having discharged many of the 1960 employees who, in retrospect, were head and shoulders above much of the trash they were expected to train in later years.

Ryan Conway and Red O'Brien were the best of friends. They were promoted to foreman-inspection the same year. As new supervisors, they were placed on the second shift, and soon began to meet in local watering holes after their shifts ended at midnight. Red and Ryan hit it off immediately and soon, their wives were socializing, going on vacations together and laughing at the same idiots in the plant. Red had a limp and a crooked eye. It was difficult to tell which eye was looking at you. Red was transferred to the high-volume rim job as a production supervisor where he spent the majority of his years with MM. The rim job was the noisiest, smokiest, nastiest, meanest job in the plant for hourly and salary as well. Pressure to attain extremely high volume production schedules was continual and fierce. MM-Warren supplied around 40 percent of the rims to Mega Motors.

Red had been offered the phony carrot, as Ryan and a few others had. The offer went something like this. The supervisor's general supervisor or assistant superintendent would nonchalantly say something like, "Red, (or Ryan) we've observed the terrific job you are doing, and I just want to let you know it's been noted. There will forthcoming opportunities for advancement."

Or, "Ryan (or Red) just be patient, your time is coming."

Red and Ryan were beer lovers. They required numbing of the senses after enduring the continuous pressures of the job. If job stress had not been a valid excuse, they would come up with another good one. T. C. Whitmill, their inspection superintendent, had jokingly called the two the Gold Dust Twins.

Their experiences with certain individuals in the plant were, at times, amusing and provided comic relief from the crazy jobs. The plant had pretty much everything one would expect to see in a sinful city. There were drunks, addicts, bootleggers, loan sharks, pimps, hookers, lesbians, homosexuals, trans-genders, bigots, murderers, rapists, madmen, salesmen, Klansmen, Black Panthers, neo Nazis, and other weirdoes. If one wanted virtually anything, it was there for a price. Hell, if you wanted someone murdered, it could be arranged. If one wanted to be saved, rest assured there was no shortage of ministers and other people of the cloth.

Alcoholism was rampant at MM-Warren. Reasonable estimates are alcoholics constituted 30% of the hourly work force and 40% of salaried employees. That's many drunks putting cars and trucks together. Quality, obviously, became a problem, particularly on Monday and Friday production runs. Monday was notoriously high for absenteeism due to weekend drinking activity, and the second shift employees were paid Thursday evening creating excessive second shift absenteeism on Friday.

Although management would not admit to it, the majority of plant injuries and deaths were related to alcohol or drugs. After all, management thought, there were rules prohibiting alcohol and drug abuse. How foolish the big dogs were.

Ryan once supervised eleven employees in a production-machining department. Of the eleven, seven were certifiable, bonafide, journeyman drunks. It was a very efficient operation with an enviable safety and quality record. Ryan was one of the seven. Ryan's drunks were not stupid, as is the case with many alcoholics.

Eight

Kurt Schmidt requested a list of MM employees who had retired with total and permanent disability benefits. T&P Retirees, both hourly and salary, and their spouses, were dreadful drains on company resources. Kurt requested and received names and addresses of T&P retirees currently residing in Michigan's lower peninsula. He also asked that this list specify individuals currently between ages forty and fifty-five. Within thirty minutes, the printout of the requested material was delivered to his office. The work would now begin.

"Jumping Jesus Christ" exclaimed Karl, "three thousand three hundred T&P retirees in Michigan's lower peninsula. Unbelievable. I knew there were too many, but had no idea it was that much out of control. "

Karl did some further calculating and deduced that in addition to the three thousand three hundred retirees he had sworn to eliminate, there were another two thousand five hundred dependent spouses. Each pensioner represented an annual cost liability of between $44,000.00 and $52,000.00. Additionally, each MM plant had to set aside millions of dollars in reserves for the retirees, many of these leeches were also getting worker's disability compensation benefits in addition to their pensions. For the first time in months, Karl smiled a crooked smile, and muttered a silent prayer.

Ksiuk & Ksiuk, a marketing firm out of Lansing, Michigan, at the behest of MM regional personnel administration, mailed 3,500 registered letters, one to each MM T&P retiree informing them of a free charter moonlight cruise for them and their significant other from Detroit to Bob- Lo Island, and back to Detroit—all expenses paid, giving each the date and time of departure and arrival.

There would be no one visiting the famed island, as it had been sold to real estate developers and ceased to be an amusement park. However, the cruise was to be reminiscent of days gone by, when the Bob- Lo boats, the *S.S.*

Columbia and *S.S. Ste. Claire* cruised up and down the Detroit River with astonishing regularity. Having been fully restored since taken out of service in 1991, the *Columbia*, with a passenger capacity of more than two thousand five hundred people would again be the magnificent steam ship she once was. Her twelve hundred horsepower steam engines would easily transport all invited. All decks glistened and shone in the moonlight. The dance hall was crowded with oldsters shuffling to tunes of the forties and fifties.

Nine

Ryan and Red envied the comradeship of the rank and file. They often wished they had similar esprit de corps among the salary people, but it was not present because of a carefully designed plan by upper management who recognized the inherent danger of any group united with a common goal. Higher management kept the objectives of lower level supervision simple. Maximum production of quality parts at minimum cost.

Supervisors were paid more than their hourly employees. There had to be some incentive to leave the security the union provided. Most supervisors came from the hourly work force. The starting pay of a new supervisor was approximately 50% higher than the average of the five highest paid employees in the department, which they supervised. For example, if the average pay of five production assemblers was fifteen dollars per hour, that particular department's supervisor would be paid around twenty-two dollars per hour. This converted to a monthly salary of $3,795.00, paid bimonthly.

General supervisors in production, inspection, master mechanics, maintenance, and the material departments were paid approximately ten to 25 percent more than the supervisors that reported to them were.

Supervisors normally had twenty to thirty hourly employees reporting to them.

General supervisors had four to six supervisors under their charge. Experienced supervisors seldom annoyed their immediate supervisor, and made life quite easy for them. Inexperienced supervisors were a pain in the buttocks to their boss until they were molded into individuals needing little to no supervision. It was all a silly little game, but necessary, according to whomever were in charge.

Ryan recognized his problem was taking the charade of management and himself seriously, especially after he realized he was spinning his wheels at a low level of management. He pretended to care. After all, he needed the money and benefits.

MM did provide an adequate wage and he earned the maximum payable to sixth-level supervision.

One of his general supervisors, Tony Blevins, chastised Ryan for his lack of enthusiasm on the job. Ryan reminded Tony of how enthusiastic John F. Kennedy had been before he got wasted in Dallas, Texas. He also mentioned to Tony that Kennedy will forever be remembered as a womanizer and a decent-looking president whose head was blown off by an enthusiastic assassin.

Tony complained to his boss, an assistant superintendent named John Wood, about Ryan's attitude. Ryan told John he thought Tony was an idiot. John said, "He may be, but he can do you a lot more harm than good." Ryan respected John and, from that day forward, was determined to act the part of one who cared—at least for as long as he worked for Tony Blevins.

Ten

Kurt spent considerable time studying nautical chart data of the river and the well-charted course of Columbia. He was also a demolition expert, and had been able to stash a powerful explosive device aboard the old ship near the engine room. The C-4, one and one-third times as explosive as TNT, was powerful enough to blow a fifteen-foot-diameter hole in the belly of the ship ensuring devastation, utter destruction and rapid submersion into the cold murky waters.

Mr. Schmidt had carefully orchestrated the time and place of the explosion taking into consideration the speed of the ship, river currents, and estimated the number of casualties. Of the 3,500 letters sent to the retirees, 1771 had responded and were onboard. Kurt calculated the death toll at 1210, including most of the crew of thirty-five. There was a total of 2,150 passengers and crew members onboard.

Shortly after the steamship launched from the foot of Woodward Avenue in Detroit, the old two-hundred-foot-long ship would cruise at fourteen miles per hour in the forty-foot-deep channel headed for the once popular Bob-Lo Island. The round trip took just less than three hours.

The boarding process took just less than ninety minutes. Some of the elderly people had to be assisted up the gangplank. Some folks were in wheel chairs, but they were smiling in anticipation of the journey. Many had been on the same ship years prior when they were young and carefree. On this day, no one felt a day older than when they last took the cruise. It was an occasion to rejoice in the blending of old and present memories. For a brief period, the misery of old age forgotten.

Shortly after the launch of *SS Columbia*, the band onboard struck up tunes quite popular in the nineteen forties and fifties. Old folks were dancing as best they could, swaying to big band sounds of years gone by. Many were not keeping time to the music. Dance steps varied from two to four step and waltz-time, but all were having a glorious time.

At least eighteen seniors were marveling at the wake created by the huge engines and the turbulence created by the powerful propeller rotation, churning tons of dark frothy water at the rear of the ship.

Couples not dancing were holding hands—some embracing, as they had not done in forty plus years. Others were seen kissing like teenagers although most displaying this affection had grandchildren and great grandchildren. There was a magic onboard the *Columbia* that few could explain, but most shared in awe of the moment.

The deafening explosion occurred as planned, just as the *SS Columbia* was in the process of completing a long sweeping arc to return to Detroit from the Canadian island of Bob-Lo. Hundreds were killed instantly from the horrendous force of the blast, while hundreds more were crushed during the stampede of confusion and chaos. Most others drowned. The look on the face of those poor souls that survived for just a few moments was a hideous blend of disbelief, horror and fear.

The bold-type headlines of both major Detroit newspapers read, S.S. COLUMBIA EXPLODES, SINKS. More than 1000 PERISH. TERRORISM SUSPECTED.

Detroit News. Jerry Rubinski, one of several dozen survivors of the doomed Columbia, agreed to an interview shortly after his release from Detroit's Henry Ford hospital. I felt terrific heat and saw a big flash before I heard the noise of the explosion, was thrown off my feet, up in the air and landed on my right side on the dance floor. People were screaming, some were afire, bleeding and confused like they were in shock. Some looked like broken manikins. Others like rag dolls. One older woman was on her back still holding her metal walker and it was pointing toward the ceiling. She was dead as a doornail with a look on disbelief on her sightless eyes.

Detroit Free Press: Survivor Morris Wright, 58, of Roseville, was bruised, badly shaken and unable to accept the fact that Estelle, his wife of forty years, was unaccounted for and presumed dead following the massive explosion that destroyed and sank the old ship, *Columbia*. "She's out there, somewhere. I know they'll find her unharmed." The words were hollow—a mournful prayer.

Oakland Press. Boblo Boats, Inc. Since the inception of our cruises in the early part of the twentieth century, this marks the first loss of life aboard our ships. We, along with the countries of The United States and Canada, cannot adequately express our horror and shock at this tremendous unspeakable savagery. The *Columbia* can be rebuilt, but nothing will restore the lost lives.

Two weeks after the tragic loss of the *Columbia*, the official death toll was listed at 1886 souls including twenty-four crew members. Of the 1771 MM T&P retirees onboard the ill-fated ship, 1190 had perished, fifteen were on life support, and another twenty-five hospitalized in conditions ranging from critical to grave, many suffering from burns, exposure, and shrapnel-related injuries. The loss of life was one of the highest in US history, fewer than the 9/11 terror attack on the twin towers, but more than the 1942 Japanese sneak attack on Pearl Harbor. It was another tremendous black eye for the Motor City and Michigan, both still reeling from the loss of hundreds of thousands of automobile and truck manufacturing jobs, lost forever, thanks to prearranged plans of men like Clark.

Eleven

Orchard Lake is the second largest inland lake in wealthy Oakland County, Michigan. Directly across the two-lane highway is Pine Lake, a relatively small body of water. Connected to Orchard Lake is Cass Lake, the largest lake in Oakland County. Clark and Schmidt met at the public boat rental facility on Orchard Lake, rented a fourteen-foot rowboat, and the two men soon found themselves near the center of the lake, around one hundred feet from Apple Island where Schmidt dropped anchor. Schmidt enjoyed the physical activity of rowing, but Clark appeared nervous and uncomfortable—scared actually, even though he wore the required life jacket. It was an unlikely place to discuss business, but extremely safe from uninvited eyes and ears.

Clark finally spoke in his normal nasally high-pitched whine. "Kurt, I'm pleased with the progress you've made.

"That is a significant start and I'll make the necessary transfer of funds. Let's see, twelve hundred times five thousand dollars...you've earned a tidy sum of money, Kurt."

Kurt said nothing, feeling a response was unnecessary.

"Mr. Clark, phase two of the plan is underway, " Kurt stated with pride. "As long as the bumbling idiots in charge of investigating the *Columbia* explosion think it's terrorism, we are free to proceed as planned."

Clark smiled and nodded his head in agreement. "Row the boat back to shore, Kurt." Clark hummed a few bars of "Michael, Row the Boast Ashore" as Kurt pulled the anchor up, sat down and rowed them back to the public access dock.

Kurt thought, you stupid babbling baboon. If you were not paying me so well, I'd put a cap in your ugly freckled face.

Twelve

Ryan and Red met at a topless bar on Seven Mile Road and Van Dyke Avenue after their shift ended at midnight. It was just a sleazy little bar in Detroit, but the beer was cold, and the barmaid had big tits. They had just been apprised of the elimination of COLA (Cost of living allowance) for all salaried employees. They were told, as were all salaried workers, that the funds saved because of the elimination of COLA would be shared among eligible salaried employees in the form of merit raises. Ryan and Red both knew, as any salaried employee with half a brain, the company had just screwed them and many others out of a substantial part of their compensation. COLA used to be paid like clockwork every quarter, and included in the paychecks. The last COLA payment issued salaried employees was $1,280.00 each.

This action, soon to be followed by others, was the first time many lower-level salaried employees realized Mega Motors had changed. It was just the beginning of the rape of low-level salaried people. Many naive folks still thought MM would take care of them as soon as they started selling more vehicles. More naivety.

Red and Ryan ordered the fourth and final beer of the night and watched the stretch-marked topless dancer slide her skinny body down the greasy dance pole. They had concluded their future at MM was destined to be considerably more take than given by the bean counters in charge.

The "Special early" voluntary retirement provisions of the MM salaried pension plan came as a shock to many individuals offered retirement. Quite simply stated, if one had ten years credited service and was fifty-five years old, or older, he or she could retire with a reasonably decent pension and company-paid health care for the retiree, spouse and eligible dependents.

Red and Ryan were too young to qualify for the first wave of retirements, but saw the profound effect it had on most of the retirees. Most of the Special early retirees had worked thirty years for the corporation. Most were dedicated employees, having been indoctrinated into thinking they were an essential, integral part of the team. Supervisors were told by plant managers they should look at their various departments as their own. They were entrepreneurs and completely in charge of their respective departments. The supervisors were told they could take a break—get a coffee in the cafeteria—whenever they wished. Well, reality did not allow production supervisors to take breaks. They rested at their peril. Efficiency could not be obtained sitting on one's fanny drinking coffee.

Sadly, many of the supervisors believed the malarkey uttered by one of the plant managers, Big Hal, the working man's pal. Big Hal stayed at the Warren plant just long enough for "training" then went on to bigger and better things with the corporation. Hal, to his credit, was one of the few plant managers that was not a drunk.

As Red and Ryan saw more and more of their fellow supervisors retire, it became all too clear the majority took early retirement, not because they were forced to, but because they felt rejected, no longer needed. As miserable as some of the supervisory jobs were, once the bonding ingredients of unity, purpose, and mission were destroyed, so too were the hearts and souls of these once loyal, faithful employees.

Thousands of automobile manufacturing and assembly line supervisors, and general supervisors, who toiled and battled to make the corporation wealthy and great, were expendable casualties when the true viciousness of corporate greed manifested itself.

One thing that had remained constant was the whining of Mega Motors. In good times and bad, the whine about costs only became shriller, never dissipating. It was doom and gloom. It was wringing of hands. What can we do? Poor MM.

Red and Ryan arranged a clandestine meeting in Red's basement consisting of ten other MM-Warren supervisors—most were unaware of the totality of the scam being perpetuated by MM. The consensus of the group was there was not a darn thing they could do. It was too late to unionize. The hot shots and big dogs at the corporate level had had them. Then, mild-mannered Earl Baker spoke softly. "We cannot beat them. We cannot join them. You pussies won't do anything, but I can and will." Earl downed his beer and excused himself from the meeting.

Several of the attendees nervously chuckled after Earl left; some shook their head in astonishment at his comments. It was so unlike Earl. He normally said little to nothing. He was a shy boy from the South. Ryan knew him better than most. Ryan and Red knew Earl had been a Green Beret, assigned to a Special Forces sniper team. The next scheduled work day, Earl walked into the salaried Personnel Department and tendered his resignation. He also cashed in his 401K plan and within three weeks received his payout, minus the 30 percent early withdrawal penalty. He netted $182,000.00.

Thirteen

"Old Timers Day" was an annual event held at Detroit's Tiger Stadium. One day per season was dedicated to senior citizens. The Tigers were having a lackluster year, but the thrills of watching them play the Yankees still captivated young and old. The stadium, built in 1912, was originally named Navin Field. Later Navin Field was renamed Briggs Stadium, and, finally Tiger Stadium. The old ballpark held 53,000 fans.

Nearly one year after the tragic loss of the *SS Columbia*, five hundred MM retirees were mailed letters inviting them and their spouses to attend an "Old Timers Day" game at the stadium. MM purchased tickets, and each retiree in attendance would be given a $50.00 coupon to be used for food and beverage. MM furnished free parking in a nearby parking lot, within a short walking distance to the ballpark.

Lines of hungry people waited patiently for a Ball Park frank—a special blend of meat and spices made specifically for consumption at Tiger Stadium. They were delicious beyond description, especially when topped with mustard, ketchup and sweet relish, and chopped onions, available at a nearby table. Huge jars of condiments with pump handles and plenty of napkins were there for the taking.

Beer stands were always popular featuring Stroh's, Budweiser, and in days gone by, Goebel, Pabst and Pfeiffers. Not many young people in attendance remembered Brewster, the Goebel Rooster. Fewer yet recalled when the Stroh Brewery was located in downtown Detroit. Fire-brewed Stroh's.

In addition to the ever-busy concession stands, vendors selling hot dogs, peanuts and beer were part of the game. Ice cream on a stick tasted better at the old ball park. Peanuts were fresher. Prices of everything were much cheaper too.

Again, Ksiuk & Ksiuk sent registered letters to specific T&P retirees in Michigan's lower peninsula. Five hundred recipients indicated they would attend Saturday's afternoon game. Weather was forecast to be ideal—in the middle seventies. The group was seated in the right field reserved sections. Each was given an orange and blue Tiger/MM banner to wave during the game. Many guests felt grateful for having worked for such a terrific company. Those who questioned the sincerity of MM still felt honored to be remembered by their former employer.

The score was Detroit Tigers 5, New York Yankees 6—bottom of the sixth inning. The Tigers had loaded the bases with two men out. The count was three balls and two strikes to Alex Perez—the designated hitter. The crowd was cheering, standing on their feet, furiously waving their orange and blue MM/Tiger banners, swaying to a standing "Wave." Perez crossed himself and assumed his wide stance. The Yankees' pitcher drilled a fastball down the center of home plate- the pitch was slightly higher than planned.

Just as the sweet spot of the black bat squarely connected with the ninety-mile-per-hour fastball, an enormous explosion occurred in the center of the right field reserved sections of the old ballpark. In an instant, fans were vaporized. Body parts were propelled more than one hundred yards in every direction. Panic ensued. The Yankee players not killed or injured ran toward their dugout, only to realize the visiting team's dugout was a smoking hole of gore. The second deck in right field collapsed into the fiery furnace directly beneath it.

Total panic ensued as hundreds of confused, delirious fans were trampled to death in an effort to vacate the stadium. Others simply ran onto the field and screamed the screams of the damned. The Tiger/MM banners ignited instantly. An odor of burning flesh permeated right field. The "Corner" at Michigan and Trumbull was simply obliterated by the gigantic and terrific force of the blast. The gorgeous bluegrass was a charred field of doom. The center field flag pole was severely bent by the extreme heat. The flagpole was no longer in play. Home plate, as well as all the base bags, were unrecognizable.

A total of 1912 men, women and children perished because of the deadly blast—several hundred a consequence of the ensuing stampede. Newspaper reporters, after writing of the horrors of the day, mentioned how bizarre it was that the body count and year the stadium was built were the same. Miraculously 20,615 survived, but all bore permanent scars of the horrific event.

Of the five hundred MM retirees present, thirty lived to see another pension check. Michigan's National Guard and Federal troops were dispatched to Detroit. Code Red was activated. The US military was put on highest alert. Fighter pilots from nearby Selfridge Air National Guard circled the Detroit skies in their F-16 Fighting Falcons. President Foust offered sincere condolences and federal aid.

It was subsequently reported by anonymous government officials excessive chatter existed prior to the devastating explosion, but Detroit was considered safe from terror attacks, with its high population of Muslims in surrounding communities.

The President proclaimed, "This horrific act of terror will not go unanswered." Al Qaeda or Hamas or Hezbollah was suspect. The entire Muslim community was suspected of terrorism. Evil flourished at Tiger Stadium on "Old Timers Day."

A state of emergency was declared and a curfew implemented for Wayne, Oakland and Macomb counties. Detroit and all surrounding communities, comprising more than two million people, were paralyzed with shock and fear. Even though community leaders assured all citizens of their safety, few felt secure and most stayed home. Those who had cabins in northern Michigan fled the Detroit area. Although public schools were open, absenteeism exceeded 80 percent. More than half of the teachers did not report to work. Looting occurred in downtown Detroit. Sale of hard liquor was banned in the tri-county area. Sale of gasoline was rationed. Suicide increased alarmingly as did incidents of rape, murder and armed robbery.

Macarthur Bridge, connecting the six hundred acre island of Belle Isle to East Grand Boulevard in Detroit, was closed to the public after an undisclosed amount of explosives were discovered inside the island's casino.

Security on both the Canadian and American sides of the Ambassador Bridge, once the longest suspension bridge in America, was dramatically increased. With additional and more thorough inspections of all traffic entering Detroit from Windsor, Ontario, Canada, and vice-versa, the process of traveling across the bridge in either direction took up to four hours.

The Detroit-Windsor tunnel, the mile-long underwater tube connecting the nations of Canada and the United States under the Detroit River, was closed indefinitely.

The Detroit River railroad tunnels remained open. The north and south twin tubes connecting Detroit and Windsor, Ontario, Canada, were routinely inspected once daily.

Industry, or what was left of it, slowly stopped. Detroit, the city that had been dying, was now virtually dead. The New York Stock Exchange was temporarily shut down in advance of a huge sell-off. In spite of preparations to prevent a run on stocks, domestic automobile stocks declined in value by 50 percent. Sheldon Clark could not have been happier. *What a terrific time to buy,* he thought.

Fourteen

After Earl Baker resigned his supervisory job at MM-Warren, he packed a few things, locked up his Romeo, Michigan, condominium and headed to Jefferson City, Tennessee, his place of birth. His father, William Baker, died shortly after Earl joined the US Army. His mother, Regina Morris Baker, died of lung cancer when Earl was ten years old.

There were no other siblings and Earl inherited his dad's old house and eighty acres of rolling red clay, oak trees, weeds, azaleas, magnolias, redbud, Bartlett pear, and a beautiful southerly view of the Great Smoky Mountains. There was not a neighbor for miles, and Earl loved the serenity of silence, sights and smells of east Tennessee.

After tidying up the old homestead, he walked out into the field behind the house and set up a standard silhouette target 600 meters away. When he returned to the back of the house, he removed the Heckler & Koch PSG-1 sniper rifle from the case, inserted the standard twenty-round magazine, and placed the weapon on the compact tripod.

In a matter of seconds, Earl peered through the Hendsoldt 6x42 fixed telescopic sight, exhaled, held his breath and squeezed the trigger twenty times. He gently replaced the sniper rifle and tripod in its case and slowly walked to retrieve the target. All 7.62 x 51 mm projectiles hit the intended target—in this case, the center of the head. Twenty projectiles had made a near-perfect round pattern of less than four inches in diameter.

Earl did not miss the stress-related job at MM, but could not forget or forgive the actions of the highest members of management. He knew greed could corrupt good men, but did not realize to what extent greedy men would go to achieve power. Even though he was just a country boy, he knew right and wrong. To screw over good people for the sake of bestowing power and greed to a few that were already powerful was wrong—dead wrong.

He did not think in terms of millions of anything. He thought like a sniper. Stealth, skill, survival and death counted. This made sense. In this crazy world, the sniper mindset made plenty of sense.

Earl called his old friend Ryan in Michigan on Sunday morning. "Hey, Ryan, how are you doing?"

"Earl, old friend. How are things in Dog-Patch? " asked Ryan.

Earl responded, "Fine as wine, bro. How are things at MM-Warren?"

"Same old crap, Earl. When are you coming back? I heard they are still keeping your job open. They'll cancel the voluntary quit and consider your absence as an informal leave. All you have to do is grovel a little." Ryan awaited his reply.

"When politicians and MM brass stop lying—that's when I'll beg to work for those pricks again," said Earl.

Suddenly becoming very serious Earl said, "Ryan, I've been thinking about payback."

Ryan responded, "Pay back whom Earl? "

Earl thought a few seconds and stated, "Anyone and everyone who conceived and implemented MM's ten-year plan—that's who."

"Earl," Ryan replied, "we don't know there is a ten-year plan. It's just a rumor that the big shots are going to reduce our benefits. So far, they have only taken away COLA."

"Rumor, my butt, Ryan. Trust me. I know for a fact the plan exists, and it's more sinister than anyone could have imagined. I have proof, and, more important, I have a game plan." Earl sounded dead serious. "In order for our plan to work, I need your help as well as Red's."

Ryan said, "Earl, did you say our plan? "

"Sure did, old buddy, " Earl said with a southern twang. "We need to talk, Ryan."

"Can you show up at my house next Monday?" asked Ryan. "I'll make sure Red is here too. I'll buy extra beer."

"You can bet your ass, I'll be there," Earl replied, and then hung up the telephone.

Ryan told his wife, Mary, that Red and Earl were stopping by for a few beers Monday.

Mary said, "I'll make sure I'm not around. Your friends are nothing but disgusting drunks."

"That's not true or fair, Mary," replied Ryan.

"What's true and fair then, Ryan, is that you are a disgusting drunk. I hate you and your lousy stinking friends."

"Who pulled your chain? I thought everything was fine between us," said Ryan.

"Get a life, Ryan," Mary replied. "Things haven't been fine between us since before I made the mistake of marrying you. You think more about your big-time job at MM than you care for me."

"That's not fair, Mary. What in the world has come over you?"

"What's come over me," growled Mary, "is the realization you are a lousy husband and worse lover."

"Have you met someone else? Do you have a boyfriend?" asked Ryan.

"He's not exactly what I'd call a boy," replied Mary.

"I'm going out for the night, Ryan. I may see you tomorrow. I may not."

"Don't let the door hit you in the ass, Mary."

Fifteen

Mr. Clark, using actuarial tables, calculated the dollar value of the early demise of each T&P retiree. Using a conservative average annual cost factor of $50,000.00 per retiree, and a life expectancy of twenty plus or minus three years, a cost savings of one million dollars per retiree was to be realized. Kurt had just begun what he jokingly called "down sourcing, " resulting in 1,670 fewer retirees or a gross savings of more than 1.6 billion dollars.

Sheldon Clark said aloud to himself, Amy, my—big bonus time in the Motor City." He laughed so loud and long, his secretary, Eleanor, seated in an outer office, was shocked as she had never heard him laugh before.

Kurt met Clark at Mario's Restaurant on Second Avenue in Detroit, a supper club established in 1948 featuring excellent Italian cuisine. It was four P.M. on a Thursday and few patrons were there. Both men were drinking delicious Italian Espresso. "Well done, Kurt," spoke Clark. "Thank you," replied Kurt.

"Kurt," Clark whispered, "May I ask a favor of you? "

"Sure, " Kurt replied. "Name it."

"Phyllis, my wife," Clark stammered, "Would you, uh, er, uh, down-source her?"

"When?" asked Kurt.

"I'm flying to New York tomorrow for a meeting. Phyliss will be home alone this weekend. I'll fly back to Detroit Monday," Clark responded.

"Consider it done, Mr. Clark. I'll waive the down-sourcing fee," Kurt said, with a slight grin.

Clark handed Kurt an extra set of house keys and a slip of paper upon which the disarming code for the house alarm was written. The two men sealed the agreement with a toast.

Clark's corporate jet departed Detroit City airport Friday at 8:05 P.M.—destined for New York City, NY. He was happier than he'd been in years.

Phyliss would be terminated, at last. The kids would pretend to grieve, as Clark would. He was confident Kurt would be very innovative as to the who and why of the homicide to be. He could hardly wait to read Monday's headlines.

Monday's Detroit News and Free Press newspaper headlines read: MM CHAIRMAN'S WIFE, PHYLISS CLARK, SLAIN

Detroit News' article. Phyliss Clark, wife of MM chairman, Sheldon Clark, found shot to death in her Bloomfield Hills mansion Sunday. Mr. Clark, who was in New York on company business was contacted by authorities. He is scheduled to return to Detroit today.

Detroit Free Press article: Ms. Phyliss Clark, wife of MM chairman, a victim of foul play, was found dead by her personal trainer Sunday morning at her Bloomfield Hills estate.

Bloomfield Hills Police: No comment.

It was later concluded Ms. Clark had been killed by a single gunshot wound to the head. Projectile fragments indicated the bullet was most likely a 7.62 x 51 mm fired from a high-powered rifle. According to forensic investigators, the fatal round could have been shot from a considerable distance from the Clark home. The shot entered through a first floor sliding glass door-wall before striking Ms. Clark. She was dead before she heard the sound of breaking glass.

Sixteen

Earl pulled into Ryan's drive at 11:00 A.M. on Monday as planned. Red was there too and they all shook hands and hugged each another. Red asked, "How was your trip up from Tennessee? "

Earl answered, "Piece of cake until I crossed the Michigan state line. Then, just like clockwork, people started driving like maniacs, cutting me off—they must have seen my orange Tennessee Vols ball cap and decided to kill me." Ryan and Red laughed.

Ryan said, "Let's go into the house and have a beer."

Red said, "Let's have a bunch of beer." They all cackled.

Once situated, beers in hand, Earl asked Ryan if they were alone. Ryan said, "Hell, yes. God only knows where Mary is. She left a couple of days ago."

"Okay," Earl said. "Here's the plan. Actually, I started without you two. I had a little chore to take care of Saturday night over in Bloomfield Hills."

Ryan said, "What the hell are you talking about, Earl? You don't know anyone in Bloomfield Hills, " Red chuckled.

"Listen carefully, boys. Did y'all read the paper today? The killing of Clark's old lady? "

Both Red and Ryan nodded their heads slowly.

"You still don't understand it, do you? " said Earl. "I blew the arrogant broad away."

In unison, Ryan and Red said, "Holy shit "

"Clark is next, " stated Earl, to the horror of Red and Ryan.

Red asked, "Why did you kill Clark's old lady?"

"Cause Clark wasn't there," answered an emotionless Earl.

"Earl," said Ryan, "You can't just go around killing people."

"Of course I can," replied a confident Earl. "Look, you guys know Clark's secretary, Eleanor Brewer. At least you claim to."

Ryan stated, "Yes, I know her. I dated her for quite a while. She used to work at the Warren plant as the personnel director's secretary. What was his name? Oh, yeah. Dean Dugger. Rumor has it she let the director dork her and then transferred her to headquarters, and she ended up as Clark's executive secretary."

"I saw her drunk at her transfer party. I overheard her telling the director something to the effect that she would never tell anyone about the affair. The heartless prick told her nothing ever happened so there was nothing to tell. She realized, too late, that I overheard the conversation. So, yeah, I know her, and one of her biggest secrets."

" Then," Earl said, "you should not have a problem getting Clark's itinerary from her. I imagine Eleanor schedules pretty much everything the big dog does."

"I'll see what I can do," said a hesitant Ryan.

"Just do it," demanded Earl. "And do it soon."

Ryan expressed reservations over Earl's plan to eliminate the CEO and Chairman of Mega Motors, saying, "You can't do that, Earl "

Earl responded, "It is not just me, Ryan, it's us. We can do it together. And, it's not just Clark. It's all the pricks that had anything to do with their Plan." I have to believe there are some good, decent leaders within the corporate structure that will replace the power-seeking money grubbers we are going to eliminate. Let's have another beer."

After Earl and Red left, Ryan picked up the empties and straightened out the kitchen a bit. He opened up another beer and thought about his failing marriage. Or was it a failed marriage?

How the hell had he let Eleanor get away? She would have been the perfect wife. No, he had to play the field and let little Ryan do the thinking. Sure, Mary was a great romp in the sack—but that was a temporary thing. Eleanor had been faithful, and willing to wait while he sewed wild oats. Ryan realized marrying Mary was a big mistake a few weeks after the "I do." Now, what on earth was he going to do? It appeared his marriage was nearly over. Eleanor was gone—probably for good. Who could blame her?

Ryan did not stop to think that excessive alcohol use was, in part, to blame for his poor judgment. Alcohol was his friend. It would not leave you. It was dependable. He opened up another Stroh's and nursed it until bedtime. When bedtime came, he decided it was too early to sleep and had another beer—then another. He passed out on the couch, fully clothed and completely intoxicated.

Seventeen

Lake Ste. Claire is a gorgeous inland lake flowing into the Detroit River to the south, then to Lake Erie. To the north it's fed by the Ste. Claire River from Lake Huron. While not considered one of the Great Lakes, it is among the chain of the Great Lakes system.

Ste. Claire is an excellent freshwater fishing lake. It is twenty-six miles north to south in length and twenty-four miles east to west in breadth. It lies between Ontario, Canada, and Michigan.

It is located six miles northeast of Detroit. The average depth of the relatively shallow lake is ten feet, with a natural maximum depth of twenty-one feet, but dredged to twenty-seven feet in the navigation channel to allow for freighter passage. Being shallow, the lake churns up quick and violent storms, as many boaters can attest.

Muskellunge fishing (a member of the family of Pike) is a major attraction for anglers in Lake Ste. Claire, along with Bass, Bluegill, Perch, Salmon, Walleye, Bullhead, Trout and Sturgeon.

Six weeks after the death of Phyllis Clark, Kurt Schmidt and Sheldon Clark met on a private charter boat for Musky fishing; although the meeting had nothing to do with fishing. Clark detested fishing.

Kurt handed a sealed envelope to Mr. Clark. "Your house key and alarm code is inside."

Clark said, "I noticed you used neither. Congratulations on another job well done."

Kurt replied, congratulations are not in order. Not to me. You see, I did not kill your wife."

Astonished, Clark nearly fainted and said, "Wha-wh-what? Who did?"

"I haven't a clue," responded a mystified Kurt. Whoever shot her was a superb marksman, " he added.

"Mr. Clark, I have doubled your security guard. Until the authorities identify your wife's killer, I suggest you cancel any public appearances, and start wearing a Kevlar vest home, and going to and from work. Have you any idea who would want to kill your wife?"

Clark thought a moment and responded, "Kurt, I realize there are many disgruntled employees, both active and inactive, but I can't think of anyone who would want my wife dead, other than me."

A five-foot wave slapped the starboard side of the twenty-eight-foot cabin cruiser, the Captain informed Clark, and Kurt that inclement weather had forced him to cancel the hunt for Musky and return to shore.

Clark was nervous, confused and afraid for his life after realizing someone other than himself wanted Phyliss dead. Would he be next? He shivered as he removed the life vest from his scrawny chest.

"Kurt, I'm scared," Clark moaned, tongue darting rapidly.

"Mr. Clark, you have nothing to fear," Kurt replied and thought, *Jesus, what a wimp.*

But even Kurt Schmidt wondered if anyone associated with Clark was truly safe.

Eighteen

"Mr. Clark's office, Eleanor speaking. How may I help you? "

"Hi El. My, you sound professional."

"Ryan?" gasped Eleanor. "How did you get this number?"

"Nothing to it," replied Ryan. "I have the MM directory."

"What do you want from me?" Eleanor asked.

"Well, let's talk about that over drinks, El. And, before you say no, just remember I know something you know I know."

"What do you want, Ryan?"

"Just meet me at The Caucus Club at seven P.M. Bring Clark's daily planner."

"Absolutely not," responded Eleanor icily.

"Another *no* and I'll hang up, El. Then my next call will be to Mrs. Dean Dugger, " replied Ryan. "You know, the wife of the personnel director you humped..."

"Wait a minute," interrupted Eleanor. "I—I can meet you."

"I'll see you then, " said Ryan.

Nineteen

Thee Detroit office of the Federal Bureau of Investigation's counter terrorism division, along with Detroit and Michigan police agencies had been unable to charge anyone or any group with the alleged terrorist activity that had resulted in the catastrophic explosion of the *SS Columbia* or the disaster at Tiger Stadium. No one, aside from a couple of internet freaks, had taken credit for the devastating carnage. Everyone from the president of the United States down to Michigan's governor and the mayor of Detroit demanded answers.

The FBI director stated, "These (Detroit) atrocities will never become cold cases. We will ultimately find and punish those responsible for the despicable crimes."

The Department of Justice warned the Muslim/American communities throughout America to be on guard against militant groups seeking unwarranted vigilante justice.

Even though it was ultimately proven, the Detroit bombings were not related to mid east terrorists, many Americans needed someone to blame. Given the 9/11 track record of Al Qaeda, suspicion of Muslims was understandable and inevitable.

The Islamic Center of Greater Toledo (Ohio) is an hour's drive from Detroit. The Toledo Mosque, with its sixty-foot dome flanked by two 135-foot minarets is an impressive sight. The octagonal prayer room was filled to its one-thousand maximum capacity when a horrific, nightmarish implosion leveled the dome and the minarets.

Simultaneously, in Detroit, and surrounding suburbs, hundreds of gasoline stations and convenience stores operated by Arab/Americans were torched and bombed. Many mosques in the Detroit area were damaged—some beyond repair. This action started a chain reaction and copycat bombings and burnings were soon occurring in every major metropolitan area in the United States.

President Foust temporally imposed martial law in several states. National Guard troops were activated to maintain peace. Looters were shot on sight.

Amazingly, Al Qaeda took credit for the disastrous attacks, claiming the Muslims killed had been Americanized, and, in the eyes of Allah, were infidels and had to be destroyed. This proved to be a tactical error by the terrorists and served to solidify not only grass-roots Americans, but moderate Muslims not only in the United States, but throughout the world.

Within two weeks, Martial law was suspended and the nation gradually returned to a post 9/11 mindset—cautious, but still optimistic about their future. Gasoline averaged $4.95 per gallon, but supplies were plentiful. Ugly small hybrid cars never did become vogue, upsetting tree-huggers and other environmentalist flakes. Real Americans loved gas-powered piston engines—the more horsepower, the better.

Twenty

David Wentz was sent to Plymouth, Michigan, ten days after the explosion of the *SS Columbia*. He had served in the Mossad for twenty years, and was considered one of Israel's top agents in covert operations and terrorism analysis. David was a member of the kidon. He was a quiet, handsome man, thorough and extremely talented. Like all members of Mossad, his loyalty to Israel was beyond question.

The Mossad, founded December 13, 1949, specialized in killing enemies of Israel who could not be brought to trial. Their actions were all for the greater good of Israel. Mossad, translated from Hebrew means Institute.

Field intelligence officers were katsas, and kidon were members of Mossad's ultra-secret assassination unit.

The Mossad also had thousands of helpers or sayanim stationed throughout the world who assisted the kidon in their killing missions.

In the nineteen-eighties, it was estimated there were more than two thousand members on the staff of the Mossad.

David was charged with determining whether or not the *SS Columbia* and subsequent Tiger Stadium disasters were related to one another and if either or both presented a threat to Israeli interests in America.

Star Bank of Israel had a vested interest in both the Detroit stadium and the *SS Columbia*, having lent significant money to each company. Wentz was held in such high esteem that he reported directly to the Director in Tel Aviv, instead of the metsada, the special operations division.

He had been unable to correlate Mideast terrorism with either tragedy, but was still determined to find an answer. He found it very interesting and worrisome that no single entity claimed responsibility for the disasters. Gloating and bragging of death and destruction was second nature to Al Qaeda.

David had worked closely with the FBI, CIA and Britain's M-16 and still had American contacts in positions that could be of considerable help.

Examination of the debris at Tiger Stadium and bits and pieces of the *SS Columbia* indicated the explosives were C-4 in both instances. Judging by the extensive damage, the C-4 had been strategically placed at both sites. Obviously, the explosions were well planned and extremely effective. There was still insufficient credible evidence linking the disasters to any specific group or groups.

Agent Wentz decided to determine who would most benefit from the crimes. He made a list of probable culprits including the world's known terror groups, feeling they would be ruled out, but still, they had the means and motive.

After spending several hours attempting to compile a list of suspects, with limited results, he decided to take a break and get a coffee and bagel at a nearby Tim Horton's which was practically empty, save the help, at 4:00 P.M..

The mug of hot rich coffee, laced with two teaspoons of sugar and enough cream to suit his taste, was delicious. The onion bagel topped with ample cream cheese was warm and wonderfully chewy.

He opened the day's edition of the Detroit News financial section, and checked the auto stock prices on the NYSE. (It seemed appropriate being near the Motor City.) David was surprised to see MM rose more than $2.00 a share since yesterday's close and was amazed after reading another article which lauded the fact that MM stocks had tripled in the past year and one-half. *Go, MM*, he thought.

Twenty-One

The Caucus Club was one of Detroit's swankiest restaurants. As Ryan's eyes adjusted to the muted light, he noticed Eleanor seated at a candle-lit table. He walked directly to her, and said, "Hi, stranger." He noticed she was nursing what appeared to be a long island iced tea—perhaps not her first of the evening.

"Hello, Ryan," Eleanor said. "Please sit down."

Ryan immediately felt a degree of shame for having threatened to expose Eleanor's affair with Dean Dugger. She had been used like so many salaried employees. Eleanor had done nothing more or less in an attempt to climb the slippery rungs of the ladder of success than many others.

After Ryan was seated, he ordered a bottle of Miller's beer and declined the frosted mug. After taking a long sip, he said, "Did you bring Clark's planner?"

"Ryan," she softly said, "I just can't do. Call Mrs. Dugger if you have to. As much as I despise Mr. Clark, I can't give his personal planner to anyone."

"Waiter," said Ryan, looking dismayed, "bring us another round, please."

Ryan had known Eleanor for years, She had been an in-plant production clerk when hired and was a terrific, reliable employee. Ryan and Eleanor had actually dated several times and had professed love for each other, then Ryan met an old flame from his childhood and before he knew it they were married.

"El," as she was known, literally worked herself up to the classification of secretary—executive, the hard way. She had no relatives pulling strings for her. Zero nepotism. She was advanced in rank simply because she earned the promotion. She was trustworthy and loyal. Ryan felt a surge of pride as she steadfastly refused to furnish the information he had threatened to blackmail her to obtain. Still, he had promised Earl, who had stepped over the line, big time, he would get Clark's itinerary for him. What a mess.

He suddenly decided to tell Eleanor the truth.

"El, Earl killed Mrs. Clark and now has sworn to assassinate Sheldon Clark and anyone else he perceives to have been responsible for the screwing over of salaried employees."

Eleanor's eyes opened wide in shock and disbelief. She said nothing. It took her a few moments to realize the seriousness of what she had just heard.

Finally, Eleanor said, "Oh, my God, Ryan. What was he thinking?"

They sat silently, drinking their drinks.

Ryan said, "El, Earl thinks he is doing us a favor by eliminating those who he feels have betrayed the corporation."

"Bartender," said Ryan, "Another round. Bring a shot of Crown with my Millers."

Eleanor said, "The same for me. This long island ice tea sucks."

"As I see it, " said Ryan, "I have to talk to Red, and then contact the authorities. I hate to be the one to turn Earl in, but don't know what else to do. I've already waited too long. I should have called the police last week, when he told Red and me what he had done."

"Well," said Eleanor, "let me run this by you, Ryan. Kurt Schmidt, Clark's head of security, used to be a cop. He's a weird duck, but I think he can be trusted. What say I run the facts by him and see what he says?"

"Now, there's a plan," replied Ryan. "Let's have another drink and discuss it. I do want Red's input."

"Absolutely," said Eleanor. "By the way, how are you going to stall Earl?"

"Beats the hell out of me," replied Ryan. "Whatever I do will have to be done soon."

"I miss being a production clerk in the plant," said Eleanor, slurring slightly.

"I miss you, El," replied Ryan, suddenly realizing he had misspoken.

Eleanor picked up on Ryan's miscue and said, "I guess we had better call it a night, Ryan."

Ryan said, "As much as I'd like to disagree, El, I'm sure you are right. Same place, same time, same day next week?"

"See you then, Ryan," said Eleanor, with a hint of remorse in her voice.

Twenty-Two

"Yo, Red," asked Ryan on his cell phone.

"What's up, Ryan? " he answered.

"Something's happened and I need to see you soon—like now."

"Hey, Ryan, since you were transferred to Personnel to a pussy sit-down job, I don't hear much from you, " Red chided.

"Cut me some slack, Red, " Ryan retorted. "You know why I'm in personnel and I've only been off the floor a few weeks."

"Yeah," Red responded. "I heard you went into rehabilitation for drinking too much, and someone felt sorry for you and gave you a cushy job."

Ryan said, "Yeah, something like that, and I don't miss you animals on the floor either."

"Right," said Red with a grin. "You will be back.."

"I hope not, old pal."

"How about meeting up at The White Ranch in an hour?"asked Ryan.

"The name's been changed to Roger's Roost, Ryan."

"Fine, Red. Whatever. See you there."

Both men were thirty minutes early and met in the Roost's parking lot. Both silently thought they were lucky guys to be friends with one another. And they were.

After ordering their usual Millers, Ryan told Red about his meeting with Eleanor, and Eleanor's suggestion to run the scenario past Kurt Schmidt, head of security at the building."

Red said, "Hey, I don't know this Schmidt guy at all."

Ryan said, "I don't either, but El says he is a stand-up guy, an ex-cop and all. She thinks he can be trusted. I value her opinion, and think we should tell her to go ahead and tell him about Earl blowing Clark's wife away. If Schmidt decides to tell the cops or even Clark himself, at least we will not have directly ratted out Earl. Besides, as far as I'm concerned, Earl stopped being our pal when he decided to start killing people. Not that I would be saddened to see Clark dusted, but I don't want you or me being involved at all."

Red said, "You always claimed to be smarter than me, Ryan. At least that's what I think you claimed. Okay, tell El I agree with her plan. Jesus, what a mess."

"Now, let's get down to some serious drinking. Wait a minute, you are not supposed to be drinking, are you, Ryan?"

"No, I'm not, Red. I quit. Bartender, two more Millers, please."

"Last call for alcohol," yelled the bartender.

"One more round, " said Ryan.

"I'm buying," said Red.

"It's your turn, you cross-eyed moron," chided Ryan. They laughed and drank and shop-talked until 2:30 A.M.

Both Red and Ryan got the silent treatment from their wives the next day, which, fortunately, for the beer-loving duo, was a Saturday. Sylvia and Mary knew from past experience, when the two "R's" went out, they would get drunk.

Twenty-Three

Karpinski's Restaurant, located on Chrysler Drive, near Detroit's New Center, was a favorite watering hole for MM Building employees. The food was reasonably good too.

Ryan took a few vacation days off and called Eleanor Monday at 10:00 A.M.

"El, what's happening?" asked Ryan.

"Ryan," whispered Eleanor, "you should not be calling here. Aren't we supposed to meet Friday at the Caucus Club?"

Ryan said, "Yeah, but I took a couple of days off, and wondered if you could meet me at Karpinski's for lunch—say around noon? It's important."

Pretending to check her schedule, Eleanor stated, "Well, I'll have to cancel a luncheon engagement, but if it's that urgent, I'll meet you."

Ryan said, "Great. See you at noon. By the way, if you leave your luncheon engagement in the refrigerator, it will keep until tomorrow."

"Smarty," replied Eleanor.

Seated at a fairly secluded corner booth at Karpinski's, each sipping a Millers, Ryan told Eleanor, "I spoke with Red about our conversation regarding Earl and Mr. Schmidt. Red concurred that, if you are still willing, to go ahead and confide what we discussed with him. Just let me know as soon as possible, after the conversation, what Schmidt said, and how he reacted."

"I thought about it some more, Ryan, and decided to ask Kurt Schmidt to meet you and me at the Caucus Club. He suggested we meet at the Dakota Inn on John R. Street. That's in a terrible part of Detroit, but he wants German chow at the Rathskeller, and I couldn't say no. But, I don't feel safe meeting him alone," said Eleanor. "I trust him with the information, but would feel much better if you were there. There's something about him—like when he looks at me, he's undressing me with his eyes."

"Understood, " replied Ryan. "They have good sauerbraten, schnitzel and sausage, and a great variety of German beer. If I don't hear from you, I'll see you Friday."

"See you then, Ryan," said Eleanor. "Bye for now."

"El?" said Ryan.

What?" said El.

"Don't take any wooden pork chops."

"You are crazy, Ryan."

Ryan responded, "Thanks, El. Bye."

The trio ordered German potato pancakes, complete with sour cream and applesauce and bratwurst on a toasted bun served with tangy, mouth-watering horseradish.

Of all the imported beer available, they chose Dortmunder on tap. It was a strong German lager, and went exceedingly well with the fare.

Kurt was enjoying the meal, conversing in German with a gentleman named Karl Kurz, the grandson of the original owner, Karl E. Kurz, who opened the Dakota Inn in 1933.

After their conversation ended, Kurt asked Eleanor, "Okay, what do you two want to discuss with me?"

Ryan replied, "First, Mr. Schmidt, I must have your word that what we are going to tell you must remain in the strictest confidence."

"Of course," said Kurt. "And, please call me Kurt."

Eleanor and Ryan exchanged nervous glances and Ryan began.

"Kurt, I know who killed Mr.Clark's wife, Phyllis."

Kurt thought a few seconds and thundered, "Why on earth are you telling me? Why have you not gone to the authorities?"

"Because, " answered Ryan nervously, "this same individual has sworn to assassinate as many top MM officials as he can, including your boss, Mr. Clark. I thought, before going to the police, I would tell you inasmuch as you are in charge of MM security. El, I mean Eleanor, values your judgment, as do I."

Kurt said, "Who is the man? Is he crazy?"

Ryan responded, "He worked at the Warren plant as a production supervisor, but got pissed off at MM for reducing salaried benefits and quit. He also said something about getting even."

Ryan went on, "We really didn't take him seriously, and sort of forgot about him, until he showed up one day saying he'd capped Mrs. Clark and intended on killing every MM big shot he could."

Ryan continued, "He was a former Special Forces sniper. His name is Earl Baker and moved to Jefferson City, Tennessee. He's in Detroit now."

"I see," said Kurt. "A hillbilly with a cause and a bad temper. I'll need this man's telephone number."

Ryan responded, "Don't sell him short, Kurt. He's a bad ass."

"I sell nothing," Kurt bellowed.

"Sorry, Kurt. Just a phrase," said a shocked Ryan.

Eleanor and Ryan again exchanged glances. Kurt said, "Listen you two. You will not tell anyone about our conversation or meeting this evening. You will not, repeat, not inform authorities of this Earl Baker or his deed or deeds to be. It is forbidden. Is that understood?"

"Yeah, but what he if contacts me or El?" asked Ryan.

"And, what if he starts killing people at MM?" asked Eleanor.

Kurt replied, "Neither of you will ever see this Earl Baker again. Neither one of you will ever mention his name to anyone again. Is that perfectly clear or must I repeat it?"

Both Eleanor and Ryan shook their heads in affirmation that they fully understand Kurt's statement. There was no mistaking the hatred, fury, and malevolence in Schmidt's eyes.

Ryan and Eleanor excused themselves for the evening, offered to pay the tab, but Kurt simply waved them off, as they were unimportant nuisances.

After Eleanor and Ryan left the Dakota Inn, Kurt called the owner, Karl, to his table and asked him if Heidi, one of the blond waitresses, was available for after-hours duty.

Karl answered, "Only if you first allow me to buy you a beer, Herr Schmidt."

Twenty-Four

David Wentz thoroughly reviewed and analyzed every minuscule bit of available data pertaining to the *Columbia* and stadium bombings. He had been able to conclude positively the attacks were not a result of foreign terrorism.

David had been trained to be incredibly complete in analysis of catastrophic events and was able to conclude the person or persons who benefitted most from the lost lives was Mega Motors Corporation, their stockholders, and executives. The value of a share of MM stock had dramatically increased since the bombings, but the thought of MM's complicity in the horror was so bizarre and incredible it nearly repulsed him to entertain the idea.

Yet, when faced with objective findings, David Wentz concluded someone within the corporation, or hired by MM, in all probability was responsible for the carnage.

Discovering who was going to be extremely difficult. To meet with anyone within MM's guarded bureaucracy was all but impossible. David knew the difficulties and dangers he would be facing.

Those responsible for death and destruction in Detroit would have little hesitation to eliminate those attempting to uncover the plot. David gave some thought of asking Mossad for additional manpower, but made a decision to go it alone, at least for a while longer.

David decided to attempt to contact the head of MM's security at MM headquarters in Detroit. It seemed the logical thing to do. MM was known to have one of the best corporate security systems in the world.

After making several calls over a period of three days—getting the usual MM run around (or the MM shuffle), David finally spoke with Kurt Schmidt's secretary, Ms. Liz Lange, who booked an appointment for David (who used an alias of Seymour Fink) with her boss, Kurt Schmidt, next week, Wednesday. Getting in MM's headquarters was more difficult than he ever imagined. David thought, *It would have been easier to schedule an audience with the Pope.*

Twenty-Five

Earl reserved a room at the Wood-Eight motel, a sleazy twenty-four unit dump clad with perma- stone and located on Detroit's side of Eight Mile Road, between Schoenherr and Gratiot. The Wood-Eight featured an eight-foot tall-sign picturing a Mexican leading a burro—significant of, "Bring Your Own Ass," he supposed. Earl rented his room for four weeks, paying one week at a time. He had no need for a telephone, and declined the use of one. Eight Mile Road is an east-west highway dividing the northern boundary of Detroit and the suburbs.

He could have afforded better lodging, but the area was to his liking with shot and beer neighborhood bars on most every corner, an abundance of hookers plying their trade often early as 5:00 A.M., but usually 8:00 A.M. was starting time. One morning Earl asked one of the prostitutes, "Hey, what are your hours?"

The lady, wearing a severely short red dress and too high stiletto heeled shoes answered, "Eight till late, Sugar. Shop's open now—want some, sweet young thang?"

Earl answered, "No thanks, maybe another time." Earl wondered how this woman could sell herself repeatedly, with all the inherent dangers of her occupation.

He sat on the cheap foam mattress of his room's double bed wondering how many times the room had been rented by the hour—or less. Then, before he allowed his mind to dwell on what God-awful things might be discovered on and inside the mattress and pillows, he focused on more pleasant things—like killing Clark.

He wondered why Ryan or Red had not called him. He gave them his cell phone number. Of course, he would still go ahead with his plan, but it would have made it much easier with Clark's schedule. *Hell,* thought Earl, *who needs them?*

Earl planned on getting up early the next morning, shaving, showering and then driving to the MM headquarters in Detroit. He had already greased the palm of a parking lot structure attendant who would allow him a terrific parking spot directly across the street from where Clark routinely parked his Cadillac Escalade in the MM executive garage at 5:50 A.M. every morning. Earl was not 100 percent sure Clark would show up tomorrow morning, but odds were in his favor.

The fatal shot would be taken from a distance of one hundred yards, plus or minus five yards. *Piece of cake,* thought Earl. He had already made his escape plans and felt confident that not only would Clark be history by tomorrow, but he would flee Detroit safely and be back home in Jefferson City, Tennessee, before 5:00 P.M.

At 3:15 A.M. Earl was awakened by three distinct raps on his door, and heard a voice saying, "Mr. Baker, you have a call in the office."

Earl grumbled, "I'm coming," put on his Levis and shoes, unlocked the three locks and opened the metal door.

Three nine mm hollow point slugs tore into Earl's forehead, and he crumpled onto the motel room commercial carpeted gray floor like an unstrung puppet. His pale lips had started to form an "Oh," and his last vision was of a v-shaped lightning bolt, then total darkness.

Kurt Schmidt slipped the Walther P-38 9 mm semiautomatic back into the black leather holster. He loved the 1942 German gun. It had been owned and used by his father, and passed onto him after Heinrich died.

The gun had been manufactured from 1938 until 1942 at the Walther plant in Zella-Mehlis, Germany. It was one of more than 1,200,000 P-38s commercially produced for the German army.

Kurt thought, *You should be proud of me, Father.* Somewhere in the dark folds of his murderous mind he heard his father whisper, *I am, my son.*

Earl's lifeless body was found by a hooker, who called 911 and Detroit homicide detectives were on the bloody scene by 6:00 A.M. The homicide investigators initially thought it was just another murder in the Motor City—probably drug related, as so many were.

When no evidence of drugs or drug paraphernalia was found in Earl's room or in his vehicle, the case started to become more interesting than a normal run of the mill dope killing. When the Heckler & Koch PSG-1, 7.62x51 sniper rifle was discovered in the room, the homicide cops became excited, and anxious to find real, hard additional evidence. And they did.

A prepaid parking structure ticket in Earl's wallet stamped with today's date was interesting. The detectives were familiar with the location of the parking garage, located directly across the street from the MM Building.

Noticing the decedent's few belongings neatly packed in a blue shaving kit and gray overnight case, it became apparent. The dead guy had planned to leave soon. A further check with the motel office manager revealed Earl had paid through yesterday's date only, and had been a guest of the Wood-Eight for nearly two weeks. He had registered using an alias and fictitious license plate number.

Of further interest was Earl's attire. He was wearing Levis, shoes with no socks, white boxer shorts and an orange T-shirt. His wallet, several hundred in cash, credit cards, change and wristwatch were still located on the scratched and battered nightstand adjacent to the bed.

Due to the violent impact of the bullets that had taken Earl's life, the back of his skull and brains was scattered in a four-foot arc between the door and the foot of the bed. Powder burns were evident on the forehead. The body was still warm, so it was correctly deduced the homicide was recent.

A thorough search was made for shell casings, but none were found. Apparently the perp or perps had picked them up.

Numerous pictures were taken of the corpse and crime scene. Eventually, the body of Earl Baker was removed and taken to the Wayne County morgue where it was refrigerated. An autopsy would be performed later. Time to tag another toe.

One of the detectives said, "And they wonder why Detroit's population is shrinking."

Twenty-Six

"Mr. Schmidt, your ten o'clock appointment is here," Liz Lange told Kurt Schmidt on the interoffice phone.

"Who is it, Liz?"

" Mr. Seymour Fink of Boblo Security Ltd.," said Liz.

Fink, Schmidt thought. *A Jew?*

"Show him in, Liz," said Schmidt.

Before Kurt Schmidt offered a seat to Seymour, he had made a determination this Fink person was a Jew. The nose profile, the flat ears, the spacing of the eyes. He seethed inside and inwardly desired to kill Mr. Fink immediately. Then, Kurt controlled his inner impulses and said, "Please take a seat, Mr. Fink. How may I help you?"

Seymour sensed the hatred and anger emanating from Schmidt's eyes, but had seen it all too often from other bigots and said, pleasantly, "Thank you, Mr. Schmidt. I'm here at the behest of my employer, Boblo Ltd., who is trying to ascertain whether or not your staff has been able to determine if one or more of the MM retirees either onboard or invited to sail on the ill-fated Columbia could have had reasons to sabotage the ship."

Schmidt, taken aback completely, tensed, reddened then loudly replied, "What did you say? Say again, Swine."

David (A.K.A. Seymour) saw the emotion in Schmidt's eyes instantly alternate from hatred to confusion then back to hatred. David was delighted.

"Mr. Schmidt," David said, "I'm here only to gather information, not to make accusations. Please don't misunderstand me."

Schmidt pointed his large right index at Seymour's chest and shouted, "Out, out now. Don't come back. Ever. Liz, show Fink out."

Feigning fear, but inwardly rejoicing, David Wentz stood up, dropped a fictitious business card off on Schmidt's desk and left the security chief's office.

On David's way down to the lobby, the inner elevator walls echoed his happy whistling of, "Whistle While You Work," as others onboard eyed him with suspicion and wonder.

Within seconds of Wentz's egress from Schmidt's office, Schmidt called Sheldon Clark and said, "Mr. Clark, we have to talk—now. No, I can't tell you on the phone."

Twenty-Seven

Ryan called his pal, Red, early Saturday evening and asked, "Red, can you get away from the war department tonight?"

Red answered, "Does a cat have an ass?"

"Red, you are the man. I'll pick you up at eight o'clock."

" Cool," said Red.

As Ryan and Red were driving south down Van Dyke Avenue, Red asked, "Where are we headed, Ryan?"

Ryan responded, "King's Lounge on Six Mile and Conant."

"Man, we haven't been there in years," replied Red. "It used to be a great titty bar."

"Still is," said Ryan.

As they pulled onto the paved parking lot of "Kings Lounge," Red said, "Hell, they must be closed. There are no lights on their sign."

"Yeah," Ryan said, "but there are cars in the parking lot."

When Ryan tried opening the door, he found it locked. Red said, "Let's go, the place is closed."

"Wait a minute," Ryan said. "Someone's coming."

A few seconds later, eyes peered through the sight glass of the door, and it was slowly opened by a very effeminate-looking man who said, "Come in, boys."

The two took a seat on stools at the bar and immediately realized the topless bar had changed hands and now was being managed by and for homosexuals. Red was beside himself and said, "Ryan, let's get the hell out of here"

"Stick around, Red," said Ryan. "The bartender said nobody would bother us unless we wanted to be bothered."

"You're sick, Ryan," muttered Red.

Next, an obviously gay blade offered to buy Ryan and Red a drink. Ryan accepted but Red declined.

Ryan was having a good old time watching men dancing closely with men, women with women, swaying to the rhythm of the music.

Red said, "I'm going to the john. If I'm not back in thirty seconds, I'm being molested by a bunch of homosexuals, and you better come and get me."

"No problem, Red, just scream if you need help," chuckled Ryan.

Red returned in exactly twenty-nine seconds, appearing nervous but unharmed.

"Let's go, Ryan," urged Red.

"Red, did you enjoy yourself?" asked Ryan.

Red replied, "Screw you. Let's go."

And, they did.

On the way home, Ryan asked Red, "Say, Red, know what I'm going to do?"

"What's that, Ryan?" responded Red.

"I'm going to tell all the guys at work you were at a queer bar if you don't buy the beer tonight at Roger's Roost."

They both laughed madly, and were still chuckling when Ryan pulled into the Roost's parking lot.

Twenty-Eight

Ryan picked his office phone up on the third ring. Mondays were notoriously busy with employees calling in for insurance papers. Ryan's lateral transfer from the plant floor to the hourly personnel section as an insurance adjuster was a blessing compared to the rigors of a production supervisor. He could finally sit on his own chair, at his desk, in his own office. *Alleluia,* thought Ryan.

"Insurance," answered Ryan.

"Ryan, it's Eleanor."

"Eleanor Rugby?" joked Ryan.

"Be serious, Ryan," said Eleanor. "I'm at work. Have you read today's paper?"

"No," said Ryan.

"Earl Baker was found shot to death at a motel in Detroit," Eleanor said.

"My God," replied Ryan. "It was just a couple of weeks ago you and I and—Oh Lord. You don't think…?"

"I don't know what to think," said a distraught Eleanor.

Ryan heard a tremendous explosion from Eleanor's end of the telephone and just as suddenly. Static, then a recorded message telling him, "Hang up the phone."

A vision of death, smoke and gore flashed across Ryan's mind. An aroma of cordite and gunpowder mysteriously tickled his nose—the face of his good friend (or was she more than a friend) was contorted in surprise and pain, pale, sad, death. "El, my sweet, sweet El…"

When Ryan's phone rang again, he nearly dropped it before answering with a nervous, high-pitched, "Hello."

"Ryan?" asked Eleanor. "It's me, I'm okay."

"You're alive. Thank God. I thought I'd lost you. I don't know what I'd do without you."

"Get a grip, Ryan. It was only a transformer that blew. It scared me witless. I dropped the phone and we lost our connection," said Eleanor.

Eleanor said, softly, "You sounded like you almost lost the love of your life."

"That's not fair, El."

"I'm sorry, Ryan. You're right. It wasn't fair," said Eleanor. *I am so glad he still cares,* she thought.

"El, I think you, Red and I need to meet somewhere and try to figure this mess out, " said Ryan.

"How about Vivio's at Eastern Market?" asked Ryan.

"Why must we always meet in bars?" asked Eleanor.

"Okay, how about Butcher's Saloon?" said Ryan.

"That's a bar too," said Eleanor.

"Fine," said Ryan. "I'll get in touch with Red and we'll meet you there tomorrow at noon."

"Where?" asked a flustered Eleanor.

"Vivio's," said Ryan. "A restaurant and bar."

"Thanks for clearing that up, Ryan. See you weirdos tomorrow," said Eleanor.

Twenty-Nine

"Mr. Clark, I am concerned," said Kurt.

"Concerned?" Clark asked.

"I was visited by a man who identified himself as a Mr. Seymour Fink of Boblo Security, Ltd. He asked a disturbing question about the *Columbia* incident. He wanted to know if MM had any suspicions that MM retirees might have had reason to sabotage the boat," Kurt said.

Clark said, "He was merely fishing, Kurt. I hope you showed him the door."

"Of course, Mr. Clark. But after he left, I made a couple of calls. There is no Boblo Security, Inc. Seymour Fink is an alias. Someone has reason to implicate MM in the *Columbia* incident."

"Impossible, " said Clark.

"Take care of it, Schmidt," ordered Clark.

"Yes, sir," replied Kurt, thinking, for a man in such a powerful position, you are a weakling and a sissy.

Schmidt, being extra cautious, had ordered two of his security staff members, both former FBI agents, to follow this Seymour Fink, or whatever his name is, and to report their findings back to him as soon as possible. He wanted to know who this man is, where he is staying, and for whom he is working.

David was totally aware he was being tailed from the moment he left Schmidt's office at the MM building. His first impression of Kurt Schmidt was that he was nothing but a blowhard bigot, but began to wonder if he had met someone he should regard with an elevated degree of caution.

Kurt's men followed David Wentz to a Holiday Inn in Plymouth. A computer check of the Impala David was driving indicated it was a fleet rental car, rented to a John Davidson of Montreal, Canada.

Upon showing FBI credentials to the Holiday Inn guest clerk and demanding guests' information on the basis of national security, it was determined Fink or Davidson had registered under the name of James Stern of Chicago, Illinois. The guest of many names was staying in room number 209, a single room with one king-sized bed. The clerk was happy to have been of assistance to the nation.

Schmidt answered his cell phone during the first ring. "Yes," Schmidt said.

"Otto here, Mr. Schmidt."

"Speak," said Schmidt.

"The man is staying in room 209 at the Plymouth Holiday Inn. He rented a Chevrolet Impala under the name of John Davidson of Montreal, and registered under the name of James Stern of Chicago. He has prepaid his room for three more weeks on a Master Card. The Master Card bank affiliate is the Bank of Tel Aviv," Otto said.

"Very interesting, Otto. Good work," said Schmidt.

"I want you and Rolfe to check into this hotel. Get a room as close to this man's room as possible. Call me if you hear him speak with anyone."

"Yes, sir," replied Otto. "Thank you, sir."

Thirty

Detroit's historic Eastern Market was crowded as Eleanor, Ryan and Red enter Vivio's at noon. The Market has been at its current location since 1891, and a typical Saturday sees 45,000 Detroiters, suburbanites, and people from out of state happily milling around and shopping for fresh fruits, vegetables, herbs, spices, nuts, candies and a variety of meats and fish. It's also known as the world's largest bedding flower market.

Red took the liberty of ordering a pitcher of Miller's beer and three frosted mugs. The waitress dropped off luncheon menus, and said she'd be back to take their food orders shortly.

Vivio's features a delicious half-pound burger made from freshly ground stewing beef with just enough added beef suet to make it tantalizingly mouth watering. The threesome ordered the burgers, medium well deluxe (with French fries and onion rings) and a cup of New England clam chowder.

After finishing their meal, Ryan ordered another pitcher of beer with three fresh frosted mugs.

Ryan asked Eleanor, "El, do you think Schmidt had anything to do with Earl's death?"

Eleanor said, "Well, he acted very strange when we saw him at the Dakota Inn. I don't know the man well, but he appears to be dangerous."

Ryan said, "That doesn't answer my question, El."

"Let's just let the police do their job, Ryan."

"Thing is, if Schmidt did whack Earl, what would keep him from doing the same to us?" replied Ryan.

"Well, why would he?" said Eleanor. "What would he gain?"

"For his silence and safety perhaps," said Ryan. "As far as he knows, you and I are the only ones that knew of Earl's intentions."

Red said, "Yeah, and I'd probably just happen to be around when he decides to eliminate you guys. I can almost feel the bullet tearing into my throat."

Eleanor said, “Please, Red.”

Ryan chimed in, “Don’t be so damn dramatic, Red. I don’t think you have anything to worry about. Then again…”

Eleanor said, “There’s more privacy at Butcher’s Saloon. Let’s go there and discuss this situation.”

Thirty-One

David had also rented the unit adjoining room 209 under another alias, disguised as a Roman Catholic priest visiting Michigan from Rome. He charged his stay using a Visa card issued and affiliated with the Bank of the Vatican. Father Thomas Crosby decided to stay in room number 211, and not visit David Wentz this evening.

David was aware his pursuers had rented room number 207, and fortunately, it did not adjoin to his room number 209. Besides, he was a Catholic priest, a least for a while, staying in room 211.

Otto and Rolfe placed a listening device on the wall separating their room from David, and listened intensely for anything they could report to Schmidt. They heard nothing.

Finally, after several hours of listening to sounds of silence, Otto called Schmidt and said, "Mr. Schmidt, he has said nothing and done nothing."

Schmidt asked, "Are you sure he is still in the room?"

Otto said, "Yes, we put an alarm device on his door that would signal us if the door was opened. I assure you he is in his room."

"Fine," said Schmidt. "Let me know if he says anything unusual, makes any calls, etc. Follow him should he leave."

Obedient Otto said, "Yes, sir, Mr. Schmidt."

Unknown to Otto and Rolfe, David Wentz left through the front door of "Father Crosby's" room minutes after Schmidt's agents walked into their room number 207. It would be a silent night for the former FBI goons.

David spent the rest of the afternoon visiting the Detroit Zoological Park, one of the nation's oldest and most stately zoos, located in Royal Oak, Michigan. He had driven there in a second automobile—one rented by Father Thomas.

Later that evening, David drove I-696 west to Telegraph Road. He located a deli and consumed a delicious warm corned beef on rye with an iced tea, he found a Ramada Inn on Northwestern Highway where he checked in for the night using, of all things, his real identification.

After showering, shaving and neatly folding his only change of everything, he sat on a comfortable chair in the room in the dark of the evening trying to sort out events of the past several weeks.

First, he admitted to himself he had probably stepped beyond the boundaries of his job assignment. His job was only to conclude whether or not the *Columbia* and stadium bombings were related and if they posed a threat to Israeli interests in America.

His gut feelings were, yes, the bombings were related, but, no, they did not pose a significant threat to Israeli interests in America. David could have booked a flight at Detroit's Metropolitan Airport for Israel as soon as tomorrow.

Instead, he called the Mossad director on a safe phone, apprised him of his findings, and requested a four-week vacation. The paid vacation was granted immediately.

The director thanked David for his outstanding work and accomplishments, then wished him well on his American vacation. He realized David would not be actually taking a vacation per se. The director, speaking on behalf of the State of Israel, said, "David, your actions, both in Israel and abroad, saved the lives of countless people, including my own. Many of the individuals you have personally either eliminated or caused to be among the nonliving were some of the world's most vicious and monstrous. Due to the very nature of your work, the public will never be fully aware of your contributions, but you can be justifiably proud in knowing that we are truly indebted to your heroism and actions."

David thanked the director, usually a man of few words, and was humbled by the great man's spoken appreciation. It was much more than a pat on the back. He simply said, "Thank you, sir," to the director and the conversation concluded.

Thirty-Two

"Just what the hell do you two think is going on?" Eleanor asked Ryan and Red.

Red just shook his head and gestured that he didn't have a clue.

Ryan said, "El, I think we are in well over our heads. Frankly, I don't know where to turn. I'm open for suggestions. The only thing that seems obvious is that too many MM people are dying under very bizarre circumstances."

Eleanor thought for a moment and said, "I thought I was such a good judge of character, but it looks like I made a big mistake with Kurt Schmidt."

It was sheer luck that David Wentz overheard two words of a guarded conversation between three Americans—two middle-aged men and a very pretty woman talking quietly, drinking beer at a table in the Butcher's Saloon at Detroit's Eastern Market. He overheard the female say, "Kurt Schmidt."

David asked the waitress to bring another pitcher of beer to their table—whatever kind they were drinking—and to put it on his tab. The waitress did as asked, and pointed David out as the doer of the good deed.

Red, Ryan and Eleanor raised their mugs in a show of appreciation to David, and he acknowledged them with the same gesture. After a brief discussion among the trio, Ryan walked over and invited David to join them and share the beer.

David introduced himself as David Wright, a businessperson from Israel, visiting the Detroit area on company affairs. Ryan and Red told David they were employed by MM-Warren and Eleanor said she worked at the MM building.

In the ensuing exchange of information, Red said he was a production supervisor. Ryan told David he worked in the Personnel Department and handled employee benefits, and Eleanor reluctantly said she was Sheldon Clark's executive secretary. Ryan also told David of his years of experience as a production and inspection supervisor on the plant floor.

David said, "Wow, I'm impressed. You all have good jobs with a great company."

The three agreed, but David sensed they were anxious about something going on at MM—something they were trying to hide, yet something they wanted to share.

David decided to take a chance and said, "Have any of you ever heard the expression, "By way of deception, thou shalt make war?"

They shook their heads indicating they had not. Ryan said, "That's a very interesting statement. It sounds biblical in nature."

David said, "Very astute, Ryan. It is biblical in nature. It is from Proverbs XXIV and is also the motto of the Mossad—Israel's equivalent of your CIA."

Eleanor, taken aback, asked, "Are you with the Mossad?"

David responded, "I'll answer your question if you will tell me why you were talking about Kurt Schmidt."

Although extremely reluctant to discuss their limited knowledge of Kurt Schmidt with a stranger, Ryan spoke for the group and said, "David, we don't know you from Adam, but you look like an honest and trustworthy man."

David responded, "I can assure you, I am, above all else, honest. My name is David Wentz . I'm an agent of the Mossad."

Ryan then, after briefly conferring with Eleanor and Red, decided to tell David about Earl Baker, and their suspicions of Kurt Schmidt.

"It seems your friend, Earl Baker, paid the ultimate price after Kurt Schmidt learned of his intentions to assassinate MM executives," said David.

"I guess that's my fault," responded Ryan.

"Our fault," said Eleanor, looking at Ryan.

"I would have done the same thing," said Red.

"Listen, the only one to blame, if my suspicions are correct, is Kurt Schmidt," said David.

"It appears he killed your friend Earl, or ordered his death," said David.

"But more alarmingly, I suspect he is involved in the slaughter of nearly two thousand innocent souls on the *SS Columbia* and at your Tiger Stadium."

Eleanor gasped and clutched her throat, while Red and Ryan gaped in horror and shock.

David went on to say, "I'm sure you would agree that most killings are based on a group or individual's desire for wealth and power. Obviously, there are other motives rooted in political or religious ideals, but primarily, money and control bring out the evil blood lust in man."

"My analysis of the two bombings mentioned has led me to conclude that, one: they were not a result of foreign terrorism, and, two, they were specifically designed to benefit MM economically. They targeted MM's legacy costs, and I would speculate we have not yet seen the end."

"Unfortunately, I have not been able to prove any of my claims, but feel in my heart of hearts, Kurt Schmidt, probably at the behest of his superiors at MM, caused the atrocities as well as the death of Earl Baker."

Eleanor said, "If I'm not mistaken, Schmidt reports directly to MM's CEO, Sheldon Clark."

Ryan said, "If what you're saying is true, David, this will destroy the entire corporation."

Red responded, "You mean we may be working for a bunch of murderers?"

David replied, "No, not a bunch, just a few evil men. In addition, I seriously doubt it will destroy MM, even if it is true. Certainly, there are many good men and women to run the corporation."

"I have a plan," David said.

"Eleanor, do you know if Clark's office is monitored with cameras and listening devices?" asked David.

"All incoming calls are recorded. A surveillance camera photographs anyone entering or leaving his office. He also has an audio recording device in the event he wants to document conversations with people he has invited into his office," explained Eleanor.

"Do you enter his office frequently?" asked David.

"Every morning, shortly before eight o'clock, I bring him a cup of hot cocoa and a glazed donut," said Eleanor. "Other than that, I seldom have one-on-one contact with him."

"No wonder he has such a wretched complexion," said Red.

They all laughed at Red's comment.

"Would you feel comfortable planting a small listening device in his office, say under the top of his desk? It's called an infinity audio device and has a battery life of fourteen days. It's slightly larger than your US quarter in diameter and twice the thickness," asked David.

"I, uh, guess so," Eleanor said.

Ryan said, "Isn't that illegal, David?"

David replied, "Only if one gets caught."

David reached into his inside suit coat pocket exposing a holstered Jericho 9 mm police special and withdrew a small plastic box containing the electronic listening device, and instructed Eleanor how to affix it to Clark's desk.

David then asked his newly acquired friends, "Say, I happen to have four tickets to the Fisher Theater tonight. *Fiddler on the Roof* is playing. Could I interest you all in joining me?"

Ryan said, "Thanks, but I have to get home to momma. She's going to think I got lost again."

Red replied, "Same here, but thanks for the offer."

Eleanor said, "I'd love to."

Ryan looked at Eleanor as though she had betrayed him, then asked himself, *What business is it of mine? Our relationship is dead. I'm married. I shouldn't care whom she sees, but I do.*

As David and Eleanor left Butcher's Saloon, Red noticed Ryan looking quite upset, pissed actually. Red knew what was eating at his friend, and knew the best thing to say was nothing at all. They finished their beer and headed home.

Thirty-Three

"What do you mean, he's not there?" screamed Kurt to Otto on the phone.

"Mr. Schmidt, he must have rented an adjoining room. He is not in either," explained Otto. "His car is still here."

"You stupid fools," said Schmidt. "He had another car."

"You and your idiot companion, Rolfe, report to the building. Go to your offices and sit. Can you two bumbling swine handle that?"

A subdued Otto meekly replied, "Yes, Mr. Schmidt."

Although Schmidt was just a young boy living in Nazi Germany, he remembered his father's pride in country and the fuhrer. He idolized his SS father and longed for the day he could don the black uniform complete with death's head insignia and lightning bolt SS's like his father, Heinrich, had so proudly worn. He recalled seeing his reflection in his father's spit-shined black jackboots and smelling the sweet aroma of his black leather officer's coat.

Kurt was mesmerized when his father would tell him about the extermination of sub-humans—how Jews and Czechs, Negroes and other forms of life were unworthy of living.

Heinrich envisioned the day when the world would speak one language—German. He believed as did the fuhrer that those willing to fight deserved to live—those unwilling should die.

The living space the fuhrer referenced in Mein Kampf most certainly meant the globe. Aryians would rule the earth.

Schmidt was furious at his agent's inability to monitor the Jew intruder who had so boldly entered his office and insolently made veiled accusations about MM's complicity in the bombings. Obviously, Kurt thought, the Jew was merely guessing, but the fact that he or anyone else dares suspect the bombings were related to MM was troubling.

If only his bumbling agents, Otto and Rolfe, could have been the Gestapo, things would have had an entirely different outcome. The Jew would have been tortured into telling everything he knew, then disposed of. Here I am, Kurt thought, working myself into a sweat over nothing—perhaps.

Kurt got up from his executive chair, walked into his private bath, looked into the mirror over the wash basin, stood at rigid attention, clicked his heels and abruptly gave a stiff-armed Nazi salute, proudly shouting, "Heil Hitler "

Thirty-Four

Red O'Brien's full name was Gerald Warren O'Brien. He was Irish as an Irish rose and likeable as an Irish setter.

Red grew up on Detroit's east side, in an area six blocks square inhabited by other Irish families. He regularly attended mass at a nearby Catholic church with his parents, Walter and Rosie, his two older brothers, and two younger sisters.

Walter was a production supervisor at the MM Gear and Axle plant in Hamtramck. Walter was a dedicated MM employee and owned nothing but MM automobiles. He was a firm believer in not biting the hand that feeds you.

Red was born with multidirectional eyesight, and, when he began to walk, a limp. It wasn't a gimpy limp so his parents overlooked it, and figured if his left eye didn't look with the right, it was God's will.

Red graduated from Detroit's Lewis Cass Technical High School—one of Detroit's finer public schools.

Red enlisted in the United States Army shortly after graduation. He had been too young for Korea, and too old for Viet Nam, but served his nation proudly.

Red was stationed in Seattle, Washington, for a brief period of time, and on a weekend furlough, borrowed a friend's car to see the sights around Seattle. He had a few brews that afternoon and was pulled over by a Seattle police officer who smelled the odor of beer on Red's breath. He said to Red, "What am I going to do with you?"

Red made the mistake of replying, "Who made your decisions before I came along?"

Red spent the night in jail.

Red married Sylvia Ulinski, a sweet girl he met in grade school. Sylvia's folks were one of the few Polish families living in Red's mostly Irish neighborhood. They dated a few months before Red enlisted in the army, and when he was discharged, married in a Catholic church. A huge Polish/Irish reception following the ceremony.

Red's father, Walter, obtained an employment application from MM Gear and Axle, and within a few days, Red was working the second shift at the "Gear," as an hourly production employee.

Red transferred to the MM-Warren plant in 1961, still an hourly employee—a job setter on the cross-shaft job. The cross shaft was forged steel machined and eventually assembled into upper control arms—metal stampings that were components of the MM front suspension system.

Within one year, Red was promoted to supervisor—inspection, where he met Ryan, and a wonderful friendship began.

Neither Red nor Ryan had cultivated sufficient people skills necessary to supervise the dozen or more bench inspectors and utility inspectors that reported to each of them.

They learned the hard way—through trial and error. It did not take them long to determine it was imperative they gain the respect of the employees that reported to them. Most of these employees were considerably older than Ryan and Red.

Realizing their employees warranted, and deserved respect, the process of gaining respect as their supervisor was less challenging, but still difficult. Each employee's needs were slightly different. Some had been indoctrinated to respond to demands—others to pleas.

Eventually, Red and Ryan learned their trades well and became excellent inspection supervisors, and even better pals. Red was transferred out of inspection into the dreaded wheel job as a production department supervisor for "training."

Thirty-Five

Eleanor and David left the Fisher Theater in great spirits, holding hands and singing, "If I Were a Rich Man."

Eleanor said to David, "I didn't know Tevre was a milkman. And I'd forgotten he and Golde had five children—all girls."

"I hope you enjoyed the musical, Eleanor. It's one of my favorites. And, not just because I'm Jewish," said David, jokingly.

"I loved it, David. I haven't been to the theater in years. Thank you so very much for taking me. I don't think Red or Ryan would have it enjoyed it. It's not their cup of tea."

"Don't take this the wrong way," David said, "but I'm rather glad just the two of us went."

David drove Eleanor back to Eastern market to get her car. She stole glances at David when she thought he wasn't looking, and he did likewise. Simultaneously, they started to ask one another, "Are you mar—?" They both laughed at their coincidental thinking.

"Tried it—didn't work out. No children. No ties, other than the Mossad," David said.

Eleanor replied, "M is my Mossad."

David pulled his rental car next to Eleanor's leased Chevy Trailblazer, shut the engine off, and she invited him to sit with her for a while. Shortly after he sat down, he stared directly into Eleanor's lake blue eyes. She felt his chocolate brown eyes cast a hypnotic spell upon her and in what could have been a choreographed move their lips touched softly, then firmly. They slid softly into the center of the front seat locked in a steamy embrace, each stroking each other's hair as one soothes a loving pet. As their kissing and breathing became deeper, so did their lust for one another. Eleanor started wiggling, but before the point of no return, Eleanor gently placed her palms on David's shoulders and said, "We are going to stop now, but I hope this will be continued at a later date."

David understood, reluctantly agreed and said, "I think you are the most beautiful woman in the world," kissing her damp palms tenderly. "I would consider it an honor to be able to continue this wonderful beginning in the near future. Good night, Eleanor."

"Good night, David," she said as he stepped out of her car and walked quickly to his Impala. She was still breathing shallow and quickly, somewhat dizzy, silently cursing herself for being such as goody-goody two-shoes, but inwardly realizing she had made the correct decision just at the nick of time.

Thirty-Six

Kurt Schmidt called Sheldon Clark early Monday morning and asked if he could see him in Sheldon's office.

Clark said, "Of course, Kurt. I have some free time now. I'll have Eleanor buzz you in."

"Eleanor," Clark said on the intercom, "Mr. Schmidt is on his way to see me. Let him in."

Eleanor said, "Will do, Mr. Clark. Will that be all?"

Clark responded, "If there had been anything else, I would have told you."

"Thank you, Mr. Clark," Eleanor replied, thinking, what a prick.

She shuddered at the thought of seeing Schmidt again. The last time she saw he was at the Dakota Inn, shortly before Earl was murdered.

Schmidt bolted into Clark's outer office brushing off Eleanor as though she didn't exist and boldly walked into Clark's office.

"Good morning, Mr. Clark," said Schmidt.

"Sit down, Kurt," replied Clark. "What did you need to see me about?"

Schmidt noticed Clark had just finished his morning's hot chocolate and glazed donut, and thought, you are a disgusting individual, and will that tongue of yours never cease darting?

"Mr. Clark, now that we are in a hiatus—as planned—before our next down-sourcing event, I wanted your input on an idea that's crossed my mind."

"Please, Schmidt, get to the point," said Clark.

"I've noticed several MM directors who continue to receive huge salaries, stock options, and bonuses."

"Your point being?" asked Clark.

"Does the corporation need them?" queried Schmidt.

"I see," said an interested Clark. "What do you propose?"

"I suggest you allow me the honor of eliminating them," replied Schmidt.

"Who and when?" asked Clark.

"Who, are four vice-presidents I've taken the liberty of identifying," said Schmidt. "The names are on this slip of paper," handing a folded sheet of paper to Clark.

"Why—they are all Jews They are excellent employees," Clark noted.

"All single Jewish men," added Schmidt.

"What am I missing here? Enlighten me, Schmidt," said Clark.

"No survivor income benefits for one. No widows to receive pension benefits for two, and, of course, should MM decide to replace them, their replacements would be paid a much-reduced salary," said Schmidt. "But, two of these individuals hold tens of thousands of shares of MM stock, have no beneficiaries meaning..."

Clark interrupted. "Their shares would revert to the corporation."

"Kurt," said a smiling Clark, "you are a genius."

"Actually," Schmidt said, "I got the idea from a Tennessee hillbilly."

They both laughed, but only Schmidt fully understood the joke.

"I will need you to arrange a flight for these four men in a corporate jet," said Schmidt.

"That's the least I can do," said a cheerful Clark.

"Eleanor," said Clark on the intercom,

"Yes, Mr.Clark."

"Contact MM Air, and then call our Michigan vice-presidents of manufacturing, labor relations, personnel, and legal and inform them they are going to Denver on urgent official business."

"When, Mr.Clark?"

"The meeting they will be attending is this Friday at eleven o'clock. They will leave Detroit Wednesday. Their itineraries will be faxed to them while they are in flight," said Clark.

"Thank you, Mr. Clark," said Eleanor.

Shortly after Schmidt left Clark's office, Liz Lange contacted Otto and Rolfe. "Mr. Schmidt wants to see you two in his office immediately."

Both were prepared to get a major ass chewing from Schmidt as a consequence of the bungling of the Seymour Fink assignment, but to their pleasant surprise, Schmidt was in a jovial mood when they entered his office.

"Sit down, gentlemen," said Schmidt.

"I may have been too harsh with you on the Fink case, but I was under a lot of pressure," said Schmidt. "I'm sure you understand."

Both men were quite relieved and for the first time in days were able to relax.

"I want both you men to accompany four vice-presidents on a business flight to Denver this Wednesday. It will officially be considered a security measure for the MM executives, but, off the record, it's nothing but a pleasure trip. Call it a token of my appreciation for your services."

Schmidt excused Rolfe, but asked Otto to stay for a moment.

"Otto," Schmidt said while sliding a green appraisal form across his desk, "sign your annual appraisal. I've given you a superior rating in all categories, making you immediately eligible for promotion and a substantial pay increase."

"Why, thank so much, Mr. Schmidt," said a shocked and exuberant Otto.

"And, Otto, when not in the presence of others, you may call me Kurt."

"Oh, thank you Mr., I mean Kurt," said a confused but happy Otto.

Otto hastily signed what he thought was his appraisal and nearly tripped on his own feet while leaving Schmidt's office. Liz wondered why Otto was grinning as widely as he left.

Thirty-Seven

Eleanor was extremely nervous Tuesday morning as she knocked on Clark's office door to bring his morning hot cocoa and glazed donuts.

He asked, "Who's there?" as he did every morning at this time, knowing full well it was Eleanor.

"It's Eleanor, with your hot cocoa and glazed donut," she answered, while rolling her eyes.

One morning, several weeks earlier, she delivered his morning treat, and said, "It's Eleanor, with your hot cocoa," and he refused to buzz the door open until she said, "hot cocoa and glazed donuts."

She entered his office with his morning snack, but before she turned around to leave, managed to affix the tiny infinity audio bug under the corner of his desk as instructed by David. She had been careful not to leave her fingerprints on the device and had stuck small strips of cellophane tape on her left thumb and forefinger. Another bit of information from David.

Clark never said, "Thank you," to Eleanor for anything so she was struck with fear when, just as she reached the office door, Clark said, "Eleanor."

She wondered, *God, did he see me put that thing under his desk? Oh, Jesus.*

"Yes, sir," she said, expecting the worst, thinking she had been busted.

"The hot cocoa is not hot, it's barely warm," whined Clark.

"Would you like another, sir?" asked a grateful Eleanor.

"No," Clark grumbled. "Just don't let it happen again."

"Of course not, sir," Eleanor responded, thinking, you miserable low life dog.

Eleanor returned to her desk, and then went to the ladies' room where she removed her cell phone and placed a call to David leaving a one word message, "Done."

Had Eleanor been one day earlier installing the device under Clark's desk, David might have had the opportunity to save the lives on the ill-fated MM Air flight scheduled to depart Detroit's Willow Run airport Wednesday.

MM Air flight number 303 left Willow Run airport on schedule Wednesday morning at nine thirty A.M. EST. Onboard was the pilot, copilot, one male flight attendant, four MM vice-presidents, Otto and Rolfe.

As the powerful corporate jet cruised at 34,000 feet over Nebraska, Otto's cell phone rang.

"Hello," said Otto, feeling quite important.

"Open the brief case," ordered Schmidt.

Yes, sir."

Otto did as instructed, and a triggering mechanism instantly ignited powerful C-4 explosives that had been planted in his brief case resulting in a catastrophic midair explosion.

Radar stations tracking MM Air 303 showed a blip, then nothing.

Wreckage was scattered over a thirty-mile area of Nebraska farm fields. The largest body part found was Otto's left leg.

The Detroit News:

> Tragedy in the Sky—MM Air 303 Explodes
>
> Newswriter, Abe Sears reports: MM Air flight 303 disappeared from radar at eleven A.M. Wednesday morning over clear Nebraska skies.
>
> Onboard were four MM executives, two members of their security detail, pilot, a copilot and flight attendant.
>
> One eyewitness claims to have seen a fireball in the sky.
>
> All aboard the ill-fated flight feared dead. MM flag flies at half-mast.

MM conducted an in-house investigation and discovered a document in Otto's Koch's desk that seemed to explain the cause of the midair explosion of MM Air 303.

The affidavit, which bore the signature of Mr. Koch, was sent to the FBI, FAA, and other pertinent authorities.

It stated the following:

To Whom It May Concern:

May God forgive me for what I have done. I do not wish to share my reasons for ending my life and the lives of those aboard, but take full responsibility. Farewell.

(Signed)
Otto Koch

Further investigation revealed Mr. Koch had been under psychiatric care for several months—diagnosed manic-depressive.

Additionally, several anti-psychotic prescription drugs were found in Otto's clothing locker. Apparently, the poor man had been under tremendous pressure. At least that was the story circulated among co-workers.

MM officials stated for the record that Otto had been a dedicated employee and mourned his passing, along with all others lost on the doomed flight.

Thirty-Eight

David called Eleanor Thursday evening and said, "Hi Eleanor."

"David, it's so nice to hear from you."

"I suppose you've seen the paper." said Eleanor. "What a shame."

"Yes, a real shame," said David. "I was looking at the pictures and names of the deceased, and noticed there were two MM security officials onboard."

"Along with the flight crew and four vice-presidents," said Eleanor.

"Eleanor, the two security people were the ones that followed me the other day."

"Oh, my God, David. Are you sure?" asked Eleanor.

"Yes, Eleanor, I'm positive," replied David.

"Pardon me for sounding dense, but are you trying to make a point?" asked Eleanor.

"Did you happen to notice three of the vice-presidents were Jewish?" said David.

"I didn't give it much thought, but yes they were," said a confused Eleanor. "I still don't understand what you're getting at."

"I'm trying to prove Schmidt's complicity with the explosion on the plane, Eleanor.

"Is there a possibility you could plant a listening device in Schmidt's office, Eleanor?" David asked.

"There's no way I can do that, David," responded Eleanor. "The only person he allows in his office is his secretary, Liz Lange, the janitor, and others by personal invitation only."

"Do you think Liz would agree to helping us out?" asked David.

"I wouldn't want to put her in that position, David. I doubt Liz thinks highly of Schmidt, but she is a dedicated MM employee, and may decide to tell Schmidt," said Eleanor.

"Okay, how well do you know the janitor?" asked David.

"Well enough to know he hates Clark," said Eleanor. "And, if he hates Clark, odds are he hates Schmidt too."

"What's the janitor's name?" David asked.

"J.D. Loving," said Eleanor.

"Would you ask him if he'd like to have a beer?" David asked.

"You mean the two of you? That sounds odd," Eleanor said.

"No, with you and me, Eleanor. Ask J.D. if he would join you and me for some beer after work tomorrow. My treat," said David. "The Butcher's Saloon is good for me."

"Me too, David. I'll ask him and let you know what he says," Eleanor said.

"Even if he doesn't come," David said, "let's you and I meet there, okay?"

"You have a date, with at least one of us," Eleanor said.

J.D. Loving, in all his Irish glory, did show up at Butcher's Saloon. Eleanor introduced him to David, and, after some minor chitchat, David decided to put most of his cards on the table.

"Mr. Loving," David said.

"Please, call me J.D., David."

"Okay, J.D., I'm an agent with Israel's Mossad, and I am investigating the possible complicity of Mr. Clark and Mr. Schmidt in the Boblo boat and Tiger Stadium bombings. Additionally, I suspect these same two characters may have been involved in the recent explosion of MM Air 303."

J.D. was dumfounded and said, "You've got to be shitting me. I knew they were mean bastards, but to kill all those innocent people? It's hard to believe. Are you sure?"

"Not 100 percent, no, but I am 95 percent certain these two are the ones. Once I ruled out foreign terrorists and the bomb fairy, the finger points to Clark and Schmidt, and perhaps others."

"Holy shit. Damn," said J.D. and he took a long pull from his bottle of Stroh's.

Eleanor chimed in, "J.D., I had and still have difficulty believing what David has told you, but two of Schmidt's goons followed David recently. He was able to ditch them, fortunately."

J.D. said, "What does that have to do with anything?"

"The goons were Otto and Rolfe. They were aboard MM 303," Eleanor said.

"I still don't see the link between the plane blowing up, the boat and stadium disasters," said J.D.

"I'm not completely sure myself, J.D. That's why I need your help," said David.

"You, a secret agent man from the Mossad, need the help of a lowly-ass janitor?" said J.D.

"First, my friend, you are not a lowly janitor. If you can do what I'm going to ask, you may be responsible for saving countless lives."

J.D. said, "You can skip the hooray fluff. What is it you want me to do?"

"Two things," said David. "Plant this listening device, called an infinity transmitter, under Schmidt's desk, and, promise me on the graves of Walter Ruether and Jimmy Hoffa you will not utter a single word of this conversation, regardless if you are willing to plant the bug or not."

"First," J.D. said, "I could give a rip about Hoffa—he was a Teamster guy. Yeah, I'll plant the bug, and keep my mouth shut. You have my word, and my word is good, actually better than good."

"Thank you, J.D.," said a grateful David.

"Yeah, you're welcome," mumbled J.D.

"Okay, you guys, seeing as we are now in this thing together, I want to tell you something personal about Clark," said J.D.

That immediately got David and Eleanor's attention, and they waited for J.D.'s input.

He then told them about the toothbrush incident.

Eleanor laughed so hard she nearly wet herself, and David, who had just swallowed a couple ounces of Stroh's, choked so badly, beer foam came out his nose.

After the laughter subsided, J.D. ordered a round of beer, but David protested saying, "Hey, it's my treat."

J.D. said, "This may come as a surprise Mr. Mossad, but thanks to overtime, and the generosity of MM, I'll make more than one hundred grand again this year. Not too shabby for a janitor, do you think? So, I think I can afford a round for my new friends."

David said, "This is the first time I've had Stroh's beer, it's not bad."

J.D. said, "Used to be made right here in Detroit. Bohemian-style fire-brewed, headache in every bottle. Plus it's better if it doesn't come out your nostrils."

"The next headache's on me," said Eleanor.

Thirty-Nine

The death claims kept rolling in. Ryan, in addition to his other assignments in personnel, administered life insurance and dependent group life insurance claims for active and retired MM-Warren employees. Ryan was multitasking long before the phrase became so overruled.

Eligible beneficiaries, sometimes accompanied with funeral home chauffeurs, arrived as early as seven A.M. Many mornings, there were as many as fifteen grieving widows waiting their turn to make application for their benefits. The chauffeurs, many from the Cockfield Funeral Home in Detroit, insisted they be part of the process, but were told by Ryan they were, in fact, not and directed to wait in the lobby. The main interest of the funeral home was to place an assignment for the cost of the funeral on the widow's application for benefits. It was a funny, but disgusting scenes.

Ryan and his boss wore black suits, jokingly called death suits, for the occasion. Sadly, they had become calloused to and accustomed to death, but acted professionally and treated the claimants with the respect they deserved.

On one occasion, Ryan saw a grieving widow, waiting her turn in the lobby eating a box full of Kentucky Fried Chicken, chasing it down with a huge orange drink at seven thirty A.M. Ryan observed the plus-sized lady had enough grease on her hands and fingers to lubricate a mid-sized automobile.

Many widows expected a check and/or cash would be handed them on the site, and were quite disappointed when apprised that the decision to pay their claim would be made by Metropolitan Life Insurance Company.

Several did not qualify as their dead spouse had failed to include them as current beneficiaries.

Some beneficiaries were actually spouses from a previous marriage. Some situations were quite laughable, while others—widows of employees Ryan had known personally were quite upsetting.

Dozens of claims were made for group dependent life insurance, and many claimants became angry when Ryan told them this benefit was paid to the employee or retiree in the event the spouse, or other dependents of the employee or retiree died. He tried, unsuccessfully in many instances, the definition of the word dependent.

Petitions were mailed from Lansing to MM for Worker's Compensation benefits. The only legitimate claims arising out of the recent disasters where those MM employees killed on flight 303. Those widows and/or widowers would receive weekly death benefits for nearly ten years—actually five hundred weeks.

Ryan was quite busy in personnel but never thought of going back to the plant as a supervisor or even as a general supervisor. He had paid his dues but still had deep respect for his fellow supervisors who were destined to spend the rest of their careers in the plant chasing parts, people and dreams. Unfortunately, many of the plant supervisors tended to resent their counterparts working in the offices, even those who had spent years on the plant floor. The resentments generally were expressed with jokes and innuendoes as opposed to genuine dislike.

He and Red could spot an experienced floor supervisor at one hundred yards. After years of pounding cement or pecan block floors, they all seemed to walk the same—their knee, hip and ankle joints were wearing out. Most had a beer belly, poor posture, a haggard looks about them and a nagging cough from a combination of cigarette smoke, oil mist, smoke from butt-welding combustion and a myriad of chemicals and oils found in the plant. Asbestos particles were known to exist in the plant atmosphere from old insulation or produced from brake shoe grinding operations.

Carcinogenic chemicals, such as trichloroethylene, once used freely by many employees were banned and removed from the premises—except for several fifty gallon drums hidden carefully by employees and supervisors who found trichloroethylene an excellent degreasing agent.

One thing working in personnel had in common with the plant was the continual backstabbing by some in an attempt to impress the bosses. It was an evil and cruel practice, but one appreciated and perpetuated by management. Backstabbing, and the subsequent information forwarded to higher supervision, was, in Ryan's view, symptomatic of weak management, decaying of once great leadership, and a sign of end-times, but there was little Ryan could do, other than keep his nose clean, and avoid getting sucked into the vicious rumor mill. He had been there and done that.

Forty

"Mr. Clark's, office," Eleanor spoke into her telephone.

"Hi El," said Ryan. "What's new?"

"Hello, Ryan, how are you?" said Eleanor.

"Doing fair." Ryan said.

"Listen, the reason I called is I have a problem, and need to talk with you," said Ryan.

"What kind of problem? " asked Eleanor.

"My wife left me, and said she isn't coming back. Said she finally found her true love," said Ryan.

"Maybe she doesn't mean it, Ryan," Eleanor responded.

"When I got home from work, the house was empty, save my clothes and a few miscellaneous items," Ryan said. "So, yeah, I think she means it."

"Ryan, I told David I'd meet him tonight and we have a dinner planned tomorrow, but…"

"That's okay, El. You don't need anyone pissing and moaning to you. You and David have a good time. Later." Ryan quickly hung up the phone.

Damn it, Ryan, Eleanor thought. *Where were you when I needed you? Just two months after we told one another how much we were in love—bang—you get married. How many years ago? Now your wife leaves you and you want to talk to me? Plus you are trying to put a guilt trip on me for seeing David. Bullshit. Oh, Ryan, why did you leave me then and why did you hang up now?*

When Eleanor met David for drinks after work, he could tell she was not herself. She kept looking at her wristwatch and seemed unusually distant.

When David asked her questions, she would answer in one-word responses, whenever possible.

He finally asked, "Eleanor, what's wrong with you?"

"Nothing," Eleanor said.

"Something is wrong," David said. "Tell me."

"If you must know, it's Ryan. He's having marital problems."

"Is that any of your concern?" David asked.

David instantly knew that was a question he should not have asked, as Eleanor's fuse suddenly blew, and she said, "You're damn right it's my concern. Ryan is my best friend. We have quite a history, thank you, and now he's hurting."

"By the way, David, you said you were not married. Are you?" asked Eleanor.

David hedged and replied, "Well, uh, er. I was going to…"

Luckily for David, Eleanor didn't have a weapon on her person, and as she was getting up to leave said, "You son of a bitch. Just the Mossad, my ass. Men." And she left the bar, went directly home and called Ryan.

Eleanor called Ryan's cell phone and was immediately directed to his answering service. Must have it off, she thought.

She then called Red, who answered on the second ring.

"Red, it's Eleanor."

"Hi, Eleanor," said Red. "What's up?"

"I tried calling Ryan, but got no answer. Do you know where he is, Red?"

"Yeah," said Red. "He's at the Roost. I left him there just a few minutes ago. And, yes, I know about his wife leaving him. Told him I'd stick around if he wanted to talk, and he told me he didn't want company."

"Drinking isn't going to help him, Red. He knows that."

"That's the thing. When I left, he was drinking Vernor's ginger ale," said Red. "That's a first for Ryan at the Roost."

"Must be really taking it hard, huh?" asked Eleanor.

Red said, "Yeah, plus he said an old friend wouldn't give him the time of day. Wasn't me. Wonder whom he was talking about?"

That really hurt, thought Eleanor as she thanked Red for the information and then headed straight to Roger's Roost.

She found Ryan seated in a corner booth in the darkest part of the Roost. On the table was a pitcher of something that resembled beer in color, but without the foamy head. She guessed it was Vernor's and she guessed correctly.

Eleanor slipped up behind him and softly said, "Ryan." He was startled to see her.

"El, I am so glad you came. I thought you had a date. How did you know I was here? I'm sorry, have a seat."

"Ryan, I'm here because this is where I'm supposed to be. Forget about my date—I have. Red told me you were here drinking ginger ale, and I really got worried."

Ryan said, "I'm drinking Vernor's because if I drink what I'd like to drink, I wouldn't know when to quit. And, it isn't only that my wife left. I don't blame her. It's just that my entire life has been a series of lousy decisions. Leaving you was lousy decision number one. Drinking too much, too often is lousy decision number two. About the only thing going right is my job, and, who knows, the way things are going, it could be outsourced to some stinking insurance company."

Elizabeth thought for a moment and said, "Ryan, we all make mistakes—that's life. We sometimes have an opportunity to make things right, but still have to live with the things we've done. The important thing is to try to make the right decisions now and leave the past where it belongs—in the past. Yes, leaving me was a very bad decision. And, I won't tell you I'll be available even if you and your wife part for good. I can tell you, there is no way I'll sleep with a married man, and I'll leave it there for you to ponder. As for your drinking, if you think you have a problem, you probably do. I've been considering quitting drinking. If you want to climb aboard the wagon, let me know. There are some very cool recovery programs out there. Finally, as for your job, you were always an excellent employee, and I doubt seriously MM will screw you too badly, even if your job is farmed out. Now, how about sharing some of that ginger ale before it goes flat?"

"Thanks, El," said Ryan. "You don't know how much you being here means to me."

"But, I do," said Eleanor.

"God, this ginger ale is sweet," said Ryan.

Soon, the conversation switched to the horrors of the near past. The tragedies of the *Columbia*, Tiger Stadium, Earl, and the latest airplane incident seemed surreal. Was David correct in placing blame on Clark and Schmidt? What was an agent of a foreign country doing here anyway? What would possess one of the most powerful leaders in the American automobile industry to suddenly become involved in mass murder? Would greed or the quest for power eradicate one's ability to differentiate right from wrong?

When Eleanor and Ryan left the Roost, they parted with many more unresolved questions than answers, but they parted friends, with a future potential for a much closer relationship.

Eleanor pecked Ryan softly on the cheek, and said, "Goodnight, Ryan"

Ryan, with no opportunity to reciprocate, simply said, "Goodnight, El. Thanks."

Forty-One

The first message David intercepted from the bugs planted in Clark's and Schmidt's offices was interesting, but gave insufficient clues as to what was on their killing agenda.

"Mr. Clark. We are a go," said Schmidt.

"A retiree's farewell, indeed," chuckled Clark. "It is another step in the right direction. Way to go, Schmidt."

"Not too many, but not an insignificant number either," said Schmidt.

"And to think they once felt they were not expendable," said Clark.

David listened carefully to the voice recordings but was unable to determine whether it referred to an evil planned event or was just talk. He had a sick feeling something terrible was likely to happen.

The salaried retirees of MM-Warren, now Warren Power-Train, met every second month for lunch at the Warren Chateau, a banquet center. It was a celebration with retirees reminiscing over good and bad times. The food was generally decent, and drinks were available, although most of the old guys and gals had given up alcohol for soft drinks or tea.

Generally, there were twenty-five to thirty salaried retirees there, but on this occasion, fifty some showed up as they were told a guest speaker would be there—Big Hal, the working man's pal, was to speak after lunch. Hal was a great speaker, now retired from his last assignment as vice-president of MM/UAW labor relation's department.

As Hal stood behind the podium, grinning like a Cheshire cat, he keyed the microphone, and before the electronic crackle, a terrific explosion killed all in the banquet room. The force of the bomb was sufficient to break all windows on the first floor putting the entire hall out of service for several weeks. The City of Warren and Center Line fire departments responded within minutes to extinguish the ensuing fire. Fifty-three retirees, three waitresses and Big Hal were killed instantly. It was the most horrific single incident the city of Warren had ever seen.

All metropolitan newspapers ran special editions, but the most compelling headlines appeared in the Macomb Daily.

> DEADLY BOMBING IN WARREN—MM TARGETED
> News about the MM family traveled quickly between employees and retirees as well. The word-gossip among these groups quickly had the death toll more than two hundred. One lady at MM's regional personnel center reported there were five hundred dead, and many more not expected to live.

The actual death toll was tragic enough. The broken lives, the distraught widows, children and grandchildren—lives forever ruined—were lives changed, never to be the same. It was heartbreak forever for the poor, weeping relatives.

Sheldon Clark made a rare television appearance expressing sympathy on behalf of the Corporation for the devastated families. He promised that the process of payment of MM insurance benefits to beneficiaries would be expedited to help those in need.

David, who was watching the special broadcast, nearly barfed after hearing Clark say, "Our thoughts and prayers are with..."

David decided it was time to have a meeting with Eleanor, Ryan, Red, and J.D. He called Eleanor at work, and after receiving a frosty exchange, Eleanor finally agreed to arrange the meeting at her townhouse in Rochester Hills.

As they took their seats in Eleanor's meticulously clean and superbly decorated townhouse, David led the conversation.

"Thank you, Eleanor, for arranging this meeting in your lovely home. Ryan, Red, J.D., I asked Eleanor to have this get-together to discuss what I know and do not know about recent events. First, the audio monitoring devices in Clark's and Schmidt's offices are working well. Unfortunately, they have not implicated themselves in any wrongdoing, but due to some comments recently made, I have strong suspicions Schmidt was involved in the bombing at the Warren banquet hall. In one week, the batteries will be useless and I would ask you, Eleanor, and you, J.D., to retrieve the devices and return them to me. Frankly, if conclusive evidence is not obtained by the time the batteries expire, I'll conclude my involvement with this matter and return to Tel Aviv."

Red said, "You mean you had us drive here so you could tell us you are giving up? That's chicken-shit."

David did not reply.

Ryan said, "He didn't say that, Red. He said if he doesn't get any useful information before the batteries die, he is going to boogie back to Israel."

"There's got to be something we can do," said J.D.

"Like what?" asked Eleanor.

"If we could get Wimpy and Hitler to suspect one another…" said J.D.

"You mean Clark and Schmidt," asked David.

"Those are the ones," replied J.D.

"You've given me an idea, J.D.," said a smiling David.

"You should have been a secret agent," said Ryan.

"Who says I'm not?" joked J.D. "I am in the TBI."

"The what?" asked Ryan.

Red, without missing a beat said, "Tooth Brush Investigation."

They all had a much-needed laugh.

"Let me work on a plan, thanks to J.D.'s idea. What I'm thinking of is editing Clark's recorded conversations and transforming his own words into statements that demean, undermine, and infuriate Schmidt. I'll burn the new recording onto a CD then all we have to do is make sure Schmidt gets a copy," said David.

"That's a hell of a great idea," said Red.

"Amen to that," chimed Ryan.

"I'll deliver the CD to Schmidt's office—right after I check out Clark's toothbrush," said J.D., looking rather proudly.

J.D. made the statement with such a straight face; it took everyone a few seconds to see the sick humor before they all roared in laughter.

As the four men were leaving, Eleanor asked Ryan if he minded staying just a few minutes. He did so, gladly.

"Ryan," said Eleanor. "How's it going? You were kind of down when I last saw you."

"I'm doing well, thanks, El. Since we talked, I've become an official member of an anonymous group—of course now it's not anonymous now 'cause I told you."

"Ryan, I'm so proud of you, I could just give you a great big hug." And she did.

"My sponsor told me to not form any new relationships for one year. How long have we known each other, El?"

"Oh, about fifteen years, give or take a year," said Eleanor.

"So, you wouldn't consider ours to be a new relationship, would you?"

"No, Ryan, not new at all," Eleanor said as she smiled.

"But," she said, "as long as you are officially married, our relationship will remain Platonic."

"Fair enough," said Ryan. "How about one Platonic kiss for the road?"

And they kissed, a long meaningful kiss.

Forty-Two

It didn't take David long to extract a few words from Clark's recorded message. Three words should drive Schmidt to the brink of insanity—wait he's already insane, thought David.

It took David less than twenty minutes to burn Clark's words onto a CD.

That should do it, thought David. Now to get in touch with J.D. Loving and get this plan in motion. David smiled, thinking of the look on Schmidt's face as he listened to the damning words of his boss, Sheldon Clark.

SCHMIDT IS EXPENDABLE

J.D. placed the CD on Schmidt's desk early the next morning, making sure his back was to the camera mounted in Kurt's office. Taped onto the jewel case that contained Clark's recording was a sealed envelope addressed to Kurt Schmidt with a brief note enclosed:

> Mr. Schmidt:
>
> Personal and confidential. For your ears only. Was Brutus a friend of Caesar's?
>
> A true friend,
> Heil Hitler

J.D. Loving was a born leader, and many that didn't know him wondered why he was a lowly janitor. He was what he was because he had no interest in anything other than being a janitor. To him it was the absolute best job in the world. As a district committeeman, he got all the overtime he wanted, and was able to represent union brothers and sisters who had been shafted by their bosses, and even those who were crummy employees still contractual rights for representation. He didn't make the waves he used to by harassing supervisors and general supervisors with grievance after grievance. The word was out to not screw with J.D. and he liked it that way.

J.D. felt that had it not been for the union, he and his fellow hourly employees would be earning a minimum wage, treated like dogs, and have no rights whatsoever. He also knew lower management benefitted as a result of the UAW and their contracts with MM. He realized that whenever union employees received a contractual wage increase, so would supervision. Of course, that was changing for supervision now as the hotshot upper shooters finally realized they simply did not have to give their lowly supervisors much of anything. The big dogs started playing hardball in the early 1980s, enacting takeaway plans from supervision that had been preplanned in the early 1970s.

He also was aware the corporation was downsizing and there wasn't much the union could do about it. It was sad to see so many jobs sent to foreign countries and sadder yet to see all the damn foreign cars on the roads. MM had simply been unable to compete with the nips, but, in J.D.'s mind, it was all a well-thought-out plan by MM to drastically change the face of American auto and truck manufacturing by claiming they simply could not compete. And, to make matters worse, MM and the other American automakers tried to blame the union for the company's woes. What a crock of shit, thought J.D.

Now, J.D. thought, the evil bastards are killing retirees. At least that's what David Wentz, really secret agent man thinks. Maybe he's right. What a scary thought. Should be interesting to see what old killer Schmidt does after listening to the CD. With any luck he'll goose step down to Clark's office and blow him away.

J.D. met Ryan at a MM/UAW quality of work seminar in Bloomington, Indiana. It was a company/union-sponsored activity to show how each side needed to work together to form a more cohesive relationship, how salary and hourly workers were really on the same team. It was such a ridiculous idea, but a great occasion to party.

Ryan and J.D. met in a bar near the conference center when they were supposed to be attending class and struck up a conversation. When J.D. discovered Ryan was a benefits administrator and Ryan found out J.D. was a district committeeman, initially each viewed the other as an enemy. Ryan jokingly called J.D. a Stalinist commie, and J.D. called Ryan a capitalist oinker. Then they laughed like hell over their silliness. They agreed they were both on a sinking ship, and mistakes had been made on both MM and the UAW's side. They also concluded they would probably make it to retirement, with a decent pension with health care provided. Both concurred. NAFTA was a stupid idea and that CAFÉ standards would hurt the auto industry.

They realized they were more alike than not, and didn't need a seminar to remind them. From that point on, the two communicated freely, exchanging ideas and swapping gossip.

Forty-Three

Clark reduced Max's wages and hours worked weeks after Phyliss was murdered. The old gardener was bitter and would have looked for other work were he not so old and lame. But, he concluded, he would stay for a while just to hassle Clark.

At first, Max continued his lawn maintenance and flower care with the same pride he had shown for some twenty-five years—when Clark's father first hired him. Max respected Clark Sr. but had no respect for his sissy-looking son, Sheldon. Max thought—Who would name their son Sheldon? Then the old gardener plotted his revenge.

At first flowers died, one at a time. They simply withered up.

Then the beautiful lawn Max so meticulously manicured for so many years developed a huge cross-like design that browned ever so slightly. Then at each end of the cross thing a shorter line appeared, but on a ninety-degree angle.

One afternoon, Clark asked Hans, "What's that on the front lawn, Max?"

Max replied, "It's a root fungus, Mr. Clark. It's being taken care of."

"And," Clark said, "The flowers aren't healthy. Give them some fertilizer or whatever you people do."

"Of course, Mr. Clark," said Max.

You people, my rear end, thought Max.

On the old gardener's last day of employment, as a going away gift and token of his appreciation, Max crept into Clark's garage and deposited his own personal pile of human excrement on the driver's seat of Clark's Cadillac SUV and thoroughly soaked the carpeted floor mats with his acrid, odorous, dark yellow urine.

It was going to be a beautiful late spring day in Michigan. Max stopped for a moment to gaze upon the perfect lawn and hundreds of gorgeous flowers. All the flowers were dead, brown with stems hanging limply. The lawn was perfect—except for a huge brown SWASTIKA imprinted in the middle of the grass. Rock salt has many uses, thought Max, as he limped into his '76 Chevy pickup and drove away, smiling an old man's wrinkled, devilish grin.

Forty-Four

Schmidt was at first suspicious of the letter and jewel case containing a CD. He was going to ask Liz if she knew what it was or if she had placed it there, then realized Liz was not yet at work.

Finally, curiosity compelled him to open the envelope and read the short letter. The first thing that nearly jumped from the note was the closing Heil Hitler. "What the hell?"said Schmidt.

What's all this crap about Brutus and Caesar? Schmidt thought.

Then he popped the CD into his player and heard the three words.

SCHMIDT IS EXPENDABLE

There was no mistaking. It was Clark's voice. No one could sound that whiny. Schmidt was furious, filled with hatred and a sudden desire to murder Clark and anyone else near his office. Then he remembered what his father had told him about thinking things out thoroughly before taking action."Count to ten," Father used to say.

Schmidt trusted absolutely no one. His SS father had taught him well. Unknown to Clark, every conversation between the two of them had been recorded. True, their words would be damning, but Schmidt's favorite was, "My wife, Phyllis, would you, uh, er, uh, down-source her?"

If wimpy wanted to play hardball, Kurt thought, he wouldn't make it to first base. Who in the hell was Clark talking to when he said I was expendable? Additionally, he thought, who recorded the conversation?

Schmidt decided to take no action against Clark, at least for the time being. He did, however, make an addendum to his last will and testament revealing his role in the Legacy Solution, and thoroughly implicated Clark, enclosing a key to his safe box that held all his recordings, including the most recent threat against his life and, of course, Clark's verbal request to have his wife killed.

For added protection against bodily harm, Schmidt started wearing a Kevlar vest and became more cautious of strangers, but not quite paranoid. He was actually quite excited about the possibility of being preyed upon. He had complete faith in his ability to elude the grim reaper until his mission was accomplished. He thought so many people to kill and so little time remaining.

After Heinrich, Kurt's father, killed his German shepherd, Pupa, and caused his mother, Elsie's death, Heinrich bought Kurt another pet—a cute, furry black kitten. In a show of appreciation, Kurt tied tabbies' legs to the legs of an old wooden milk stool, which he had turned upside-down, wrapped and draped a weighted chain around the little cat's neck to prevent it from clawing and biting him and then disemboweled the tiny creature with Heinrich's straight razor. Kurt became sexually aroused as tabby shrieked and screamed during the entire killing ritual. Kurt wondered if his father had been equally as aroused.

Forty-Five

Red called his friend, Ryan, Saturday morning. Ryan could tell immediately that something was wrong, sensing it in Red's voice. Damn, something's amiss.

"Hi Ryan," said Red.

"What's wrong, Red?" asked Ryan.

"I went to the doc last week with this hacking cough. Doc said he saw something in my right lung and wants to do more tests," said Red.

"Oh, hell, Red, it's probably nothing. You quit smoking fifteen years ago, didn't you?"

"Yeah," said Red. "Doc wants to go into my lung and take a tissue sample. He said something about my blood work being abnormal, and didn't like my sudden weight loss, either."

"So, what do you think it is, Red?"

"I know what I hope it isn't, Ryan."

"When are you going for the lung biopsy?" asked Ryan.

"Wednesday morning at William Beaumont in Royal Oak," answered Red.

"Want me to go with you?" asked Ryan.

"No thanks, wife's going. Thanks anyway.

"Keep your fingers crossed for me pal," asked Red.

"Try not to worry, Red. I'm thinking it isn't anything," said Ryan, hoping his concern didn't reveal itself in his voice.

"Later, pal," said a worried Red.

"Later, Red."

For the first time in many moons, Red and Ryan prayed that night before going to sleep.

Several days after the biopsy, Red got a call from his doctor's office. He was given a date and time to see a surgeon. The biopsy determined Red had a plum-sized malignant tumor in the lower lobe of his right lung. His internal medicine doctor referred him to a surgeon.

The surgeon tried to comfort Red, assuring him the lesion was operable.

The surgeon removed the lower lobe of Red's right lung. After Red was brought back to his room, the surgeon walked in and told Red the operation was indeed successful. He got it all. He told Red he'd be out of bed in less than a week. Red's wife, five kids and Ryan were there, waiting in his hospital room.

Red was indeed up and about. He had an appointment with an oncologist and was advised chemotherapy would not be necessary. Radiation would not be needed. He was told to take four weeks off work and see his internal medicine doctor in two months. Red dodged the bullet.

He felt so fortunate to be alive. He and his family started attending the local Catholic Church, Saint Marks. He even gave up drinking. What he didn't give up was his friendship with Ryan. Ryan was ecstatic over Red's good news. After Red fully recovered, he and Ryan met for coffee at a local Elias Brothers Big Boy restaurant and talked for nearly two hours. They indeed had much to be grateful for.

Forty-Six

David called J.D. at home and said, "J.D., the lithium batteries in the bugs will expire in two days, and I'd like to know if you would pick them up out of Clark and Schmidt's office after they are no longer useful."

"Are you getting anything beneficial?" asked J.D.

"Not really," replied David. "Mainly innuendos. Nothing specific. There's always today and tomorrow, but I doubt they'll slip up. They haven't yet."

"Real shame. Sure, I'll pick them up." I'll call you and we can arrange a meeting place, " said J.D. "Maybe we can invite Eleanor, Ryan and Red. "

"That sounds good," David said.

"David?" asked J.D.

"Yes?"

"This is a safe line isn't it?" asked J.D.

"As you Americans say, does a bear shit in the woods?" responded David.

J.D. chuckled. "David, you're the big bad spy guy. Why don't you just shoot Alice and the Nazi and put them out of our misery?"

David asked, "You mean Clark and Schmidt?"

"Who else?" said J.D.

"There you go again, reading my thoughts. You must be psychic," said David, amazed at the logic and humor of one strange character, J.D. Loving.

J.D. couldn't quite figure out if David was joking or not. David was different. Of course, so was J.D. He hoped he wasn't kidding.

David did not tell J.D. that he had been giving serious consideration to killing Clark and Schmidt. The world would be better off without them. He had not ruled it out, or in—yet. Alice and the Nazi? David laughed out loud.

David continued to monitor the recording devices in Clark and Schmidt's office. Nothing. He did overhear Schmidt place a call to someone called Helen.

"Holly," said Schmidt. "Send Monique tonight. I don't care if she wants to come or not. Send her. Is that clear? Five hundred dollars? I'm not buying her,

I'm renting her. That's more like it. No, I will not promise to not damage the goods. Just do your job, or I'll do mine to your infidel children."

What a sick, perverted animal, David thought. Although David had little sympathy for prostitutes, he abhorred anyone who physically abused others. Torture, was what it was. Schmidt was no different from the German SS who slaughtered millions of Jews in the 1930s and 1940s.

Forty-Seven

David had done his homework on Schmidt's father, Heinrich, and knew of his killing sprees at Auschwitz-Birkenau and Treblinka. While many of the SS maniacs viewed the elimination of Jews as part of their jobs, Heinrich Schmidt, according to witnesses, took immense pleasure in personally partaking of the carnage. He also took motion pictures of Jews in their final moments after breathing deadly fumes of the cyanide-based gas, Zyclon-B, in what was supposed to be a cleansing shower. Heinrich watched these gory scenes repeatedly in his quarters—sometimes accompanied by daughters of the victims. He laughed uncontrollably as the young females screamed in agony, watching their parents gasping and contorting in their final moments. It was then he forced the young girls to perform unholy sex acts that usually culminated in their death.

The most brutal and disgusting act is almost too horrible to discuss. On several occasions, Heinrich would order the death of a healthy young Jew, by way of gunshot. He then directed the camp butcher to cut up the corpse, as though it were a pig, into certain cuts of meat—chops, roasts, steaks, etc. The miscellaneous parts were then ground into sausage, bratwurst, knockwurst, and seasoned accordingly. Heinrich especially liked spare ribs, and shared them with no one.

One evening, he invited a middle-aged Jewish couple to his quarters to join him for supper. His chef had prepared a platter of roasted potatoes and carrots served neatly around a delicious rump roast. The meal was quite superb, complete with wine, dark Jewish bread and fresh creamery butter.

The couple, new to the camp, were apprehensive at first, but Heinrich, dressed in his finest SS uniform, was quite hospitable, telling them their living conditions would soon improve dramatically. The war was ending soon. The allies had been defeated, and soon all prisoners would be released. He tried to assure them most other Jews had been detained solely for their own safety against allied bombers. The death of Jews in the camps was simply propaganda.

Then, Heinrich told the couple he had a surprise for them.

"You have a son, no?"asked Heinrich in a caring tone.

"Yes, we do, a fourteen-year-old boy," said a smiling father. "He was taken away from us by the Gestapo."

"He is a wonderful boy," added the mother. "I'm sure you would like him. We miss him so much."

"I did like him, very much, and I'd like you to see him," said Heinrich.

"Actually, I've put the cart before the horse," grinned Heinrich.

"Oh, that would be wonderful," the confused father said.

"When can we see him?" asked the mother.

"Well, you've already seen him, at least part of him. You just ate him," said Heinrich, who then burped loudly, savoring the sweet, pungent flavor and aroma of young human flesh as he roared with laughter.

The parents looked at each another in horror and disbelief, then started screaming insanely. The father lurched across the table toward Heinrich, but Heinrich had anticipated this clumsy aggression and calmly picked his P-38 up from beneath his dinner napkin and shot him in the right eye. As he slumped forward onto the dining table, a second shot rang out striking his wife in the left ear. She fell on top of her husband. The shocked expressions on their dead faces pleased Heinrich immensely.

"Guard," shouted Heinrich. "Take out the Jewish trash."

Forty-Eight

Holly didn't like being referred to as "Whorehouse Holly" but, like it or not, that was how she was known in and around Detroit. She ran a profitable dating service, and if her girls got laid for cash, it was no skin off her nose—so long as the girls understood who got half the money. Holly provided a place for them to stay, if they needed it, medical care, and a shoulder to cry on. She even had a 401k for her women.

Holly had strict standards for women in her employ. They had to be eighteen or older, drug-free and damn good lookers. She provided birth control devices and pills but, should one of her girls mysteriously get knocked up, aside from an ass chewing, she even paid for the cost of prenatal care and delivery. But, it was a one-time thing. If a girl got pregnant twice, she was out of the business—fired. No exceptions.

Holly had been an outstanding performing artist at the old Stone Burlesque theater on Woodward Avenue in Detroit. Her stage name was Hot Holly and she indeed lived up to her name on stage. She had been an extremely attractive woman with a figure to die for—natural blond, and had perfected a dance routine both seductive and simmering. Nudity was prohibited in those days. More was left to one's imagination than shown. In many ways it was much sexier than the show-all, topless, bottomless, mindless, so-called exotic drug-crazed dancers of today.

She lived with her stage manager for several years, and she bore him two lovely girls. He became bored with her and the children and left, looking for greener pastures, where the cows had no calves. A good riddance, she thought.

She had been offered top billing at the infamous Jason's Lounge in Windsor, Ontario, Canada, with a huge salary, but declined and retired from dancing at the ripe old age of thirty-two and then, in her prime, opened up her dating service.

Holly was still a looker at forty-five, but was not a participant in the service. As an administrator/owner she had become quite wealthy—not exactly a respected member of the community, but rather envied by many for her material possessions. Unless you lived in a cave, one knew what Holly did for a living.

While most of her clients were prominent businesspersons—some very well off financially—a few were despicable characters. She would simply withdraw her services from the losers, once her girls complained. Few had reason to gripe.

One particularly evil client was Kurt Schmidt. He roughed up one of the girls who complained to Holly and when Holly told Schmidt she would no longer provide the service, but she awoke the next day to find her Buick's four tires slashed and a Detroit police car leaving the scene. At first, she didn't suspect Schmidt, but later that day he called and threatened to contact the police regarding her operating an illegal prostitution ring cleverly disguised as a dating service.

Then he told her that the police had already been to her house, and had paid her Buick a visit. Holly relented.

Holly called Monique into her office and told her the limo would pick her up this evening at eight o'clock and she would be taken to Schmidt's house.

"But, I thought you said I wouldn't have to go back," Monique protested.

Holly said, "He made a personal request for you, and even offered to pay four hundred, instead of the usual three. A working girl can't turn that down."

"He scares me, Holly. He wears that old German steel helmet and boots, I think they are called jackboots, and he is just simply weird. He talks funnily—German I think, and insists I bite him until I draw blood on his, you know, thing—meanwhile wearing a small chain with an iron cross hanging on his penis."

"Please, Monique, do it for me," pleaded Holly. "I promise this will be the last time."

"Well, okay, but no more with this sick puppy. This is it. I'll do it just for you."

"Thanks, Monique, I appreciate it," said Holly. "You won't regret it. I promise."

Forty-Nine

The four met at the Log Cabin bar, across from Lakeville Lake in Leonard, Michigan. Red and Ryan ordered a Sprite, Eleanor a Diet Coke, J.D. and David, a Stroh's beer.

David, after taking a swig of beer, said, "Well, gang, I'm afraid the bugs did not provide anything useful. The last thing recorded was Schmidt calling a cat house named Holly's."

J.D. said, "Oh, hell yeah, Whorehouse Holly. Everyone knows about Holly. Well, I mean I heard it through the vine."

"Sure you did," said Red.

They all laughed.

"And, yesterday, I received orders from my director to report home on the next available flight—home being Tel Aviv," said David, obviously unhappy with the directive.

"Ain't that a bitch," said Red. "That wouldn't happen if you were unionized."

"I suppose not," David said, smiling broadly.

"So, you're leaving us high and dry," commented J.D.

Ryan and Eleanor, holding hands, simply shook their heads slowly. "Oh no."

"If this were the old wild west, I'd simply put a hole in each of the bad guys," said David. "But it isn't, and I can't do much of anything now. If it's any consolation, Clark and Schmidt will slip up or turn on each another eventually."

"But, until then, how many more people will die?" asked Eleanor.

"I don't know," said David.

They sat around the Log Cabin for another half-hour, saying little.

David was first to leave, shaking hands firmly with his American friends.

After David left, Red, Ryan, Eleanor and J.D. looked as if they had lost their best friend. It was as though a dark cloud had settled over their table.

Fifty

Liz Lange would turn sixty-two next year, and would retire from MM. She had been with the corporation since graduating from high school, and was as high as she could get on the ladder. She would have nearly forty-four years of credited service, and had thought of retiring for the past ten years.

Liz was a plain-looking woman—never married. She did not have a single male suitor in high school, and many of the smart-ass boys called her "Lizard." She concluded at an early age that she didn't need men. She kept fresh batteries in her house. No need for a sorry undependable man.

She kept and bred German shepherds, and sold registered pups for a healthy profit. Her dogs appreciated and loved her. That was all she needed.

She had an occasional snort of cognac, and loved blues music. She had cd remakes of music by Jimmy Reed, Robert Johnson, Howling Wolf, Willie Dixon, Son House, John Lee Hooker, and others. She especially liked the lyrics of an anonymous blues author.

> Big bone woman walking down the street
> Big bone woman walking down the street
> Won't walk long cause she need to eat
>
> Love corn dogs, love that whisky too
> Love corn dogs, love that whisky too
> Watch out boys, she walk all over you

One more year and they can all kiss my old ugly ass goodbye, thought Liz. I'll have a pension, reduced social security benefits, health insurance and my animals, cognac and the blues. It don't get no better.

She never could or wanted to figure out her boss, Kurt Schmidt. He was punctual, dressed nicely—wore a lot of black. He was not a demanding boss.

You just did what he wanted and did it timely, and made no mistakes. He would probably replace her with a young tight-bodied thing, she conjectured. A good looker too. Maybe he'd even have his way with her in his office. These young ones would do that—screw the boss. One more year and they can breed until their toenails fall off.

Fifty-One

Six months had elapsed since MM Air 303 exploded, and while the investigation continued, Otto appeared to be the one lone cause of the disaster. Ryan wondered if it was that simple. Why would Otto, whatever his last name was, do such an unspeakable thing? It made little sense. Ryan's telephone rang and he received the worst news imaginable.

"Ryan," Red said.

"Hey, Red, what's happening, old pal?"

Then Red started crying, voice cracking, hardly able to speak.

"Red, what's wrong?"

"I've... got...brain cancer," said a devastated Red.

"Oh shit. But, I, uh, thought, they got it all, Red."

"So did I, Ryan. So did I."

"Jesus, Red. What are they going to do?"

"Right now, I'm on a bunch of steroids. My head looks like a medicine ball."

"I'll come over, Red. Be there in a few minutes."

"No, don't," said Red. "Wait a few weeks. After chemotherapy. I don't want to see anyone this way. I guess I mean I don't want anyone seeing me."

Ryan didn't know what to say. "You'll beat it, Red. I know you will, old pal."

"Sure," said Red, and hung up the phone.

For the first time in months, Ryan felt like drinking, but called Eleanor instead.

"Mr. Clark's office, Eleanor speaking."

"El, it's Ryan."

"Hi, Ryan. What's new with you?" asked a cheerful Eleanor.

"I just talked with Red. He's got brain cancer. Apparently, it metastasized from his lung. God damn lying ass doctors."

"Oh, Ryan, I'm so sorry. I know he's your best friend. What can I do?"

"That's just it, El. There's nothing we can do."

"We can pray, Ryan, we can pray."

And they prayed.

Red died three months after he and Ryan talked. Ryan and Eleanor visited the funeral home twice. Red's wife, Sylvia, was in a state of shock. Four of the kids were standing near the casket in disbelief and the oldest son was in a complete denial. He laid his head and hands on his father's chest moaned and cried. "Dad, Dad, please come back. Dad, I love you. Don't leave."

The scene was incredibly sad. It was heart wrenching and all other descriptive words—none adequate. Red had many friends—mostly work mates. Fellow supervisors and hourly employees stood in line to pay tribute to a wonderful man.

Red's head was still quite swollen from steroids and God knows what else. He did not deserve this kind of death.

Ryan felt like punching the lights out of people who said "He's in a better place" or "He looks so good."

Ryan thought, what's better than being alive with a loving, caring family?

Eleanor and Ryan left the funeral home and drove and drove. They were not thirsty or hungry. They were angry and depressed.

Fifty-Two

Ryan had never given much thought to MM's board of directors. He knew there were twelve of them—thirteen counting the CEO, Clark. He always figured they were a gang of rich individuals, former fat cats of other companies, who decided if MM was making enough money, or, quite simply, they figured how to pacify the lowly shareholders and how best to make fat cats fatter.

Not a single board member had a clue about manufacturing, product assembly or design. For the most part, they were filthy rich republicans with a sprinkling of diversity having a minority or two and a female onboard to give the appearance of political correctness.

Ryan called Eleanor and asked what she thought about an open letter to the board expressing concern and suspicion over the loss of so many MM retirees in the recent unsolved bombings.

Eleanor thought a while, and told Ryan it probably wouldn't accomplish much, but if he wrote a rough draft, she would proof it, and they, along with J.D., could decide whether or not it should be presented to the board. Eleanor was good with words.

Ryan decided he would spend some time on his home computer, and come up with a letter to MM's board of directors. Hell, it beat sitting around waiting for the next bomb to explode. He also thought about sending a copy of the letter to the president of the UAW, or perhaps a copy to all the Michigan UAW locals. He would discuss the distribution with El and J.D. One thing for sure, Ryan thought, it would have to be anonymously submitted.

Ryan worked on the letter for nearly a week before he was satisfied with the content. Eleanor would make necessary modifications and improvements and J.D. could give his input too.

The three met at Ryan's house and he brewed a pot of coffee in his Mr. Coffee, one of the few appliances his ex hadn't confiscated. Eleanor took her coffee black, and Ryan had his java with two teaspoons of sugar and a heaping teaspoon of a powdered creamer in a black mug that said, "Shit Happens." He uncapped an Icehouse beer for J.D. who drank straight out of the bottle.

Ryan handed a copy of the letter to Eleanor and J.D. and kept a copy for himself. They slowly read the draft of the letter addressed to GM's board of directors.

Mega Motors Corporation
Board of Directors
Mega Motors Building
Detroit, Michigan 48200
Re: The Legacy Solution

To Whom it May Concern:

It is incredulous to fathom the means some employ to gain profit for a Fortune 500 company. As directors of one of the world's largest corporations, have you not considered the correlation of drastically increased profits with the recent reduction of legacy costs?

It's nauseating to contemplate how you or your fellow directors could condone or be part of deliberate cold-blooded murder of MM employees or retirees for profit. Surely, you directors on the board must be aware of the recent atrocities. The *SS Columbia*, Tiger Stadium and the Warren Chateau. Coincidences? I think not. If you or your associate directors value human life over profit and power, I would plead that you identify and remove the guilty party from the board. Sadly, if you take no action, I fear additional lives will be lost.

Respectfully,
Anonymous

Eleanor was the first to comment, saying, "Well, it's not exactly Pulitzer Prize-winning material, but it sends the message."

J.D. said, "Looks, good to me, Ryan. The only suggestion I would have is to put Schmidt's return address on the envelope. And, just in case, make sure there are no fingerprints on the letter or envelope."

"In addition, don't lick the glue on the envelope. Someone might try for a DNA check," added Eleanor.

"Sounds like a stretch," said Ryan, "but I'll seal it with water or get one of those self-sticking envelopes."

"Ryan," asked Eleanor, "do you think anyone will react to the letter?"

"Sure," answered Ryan. "They'll either send it to Schmidt or file thirteen—the shredder."

"How about the UAW, you said something about sending it to them?" asked J.D.

"That's a good question, J.D.," answered Ryan. "We'll just have to wait and see."

Fifty-Three

Monique arrived promptly at Schmidt's house at the prescheduled time. She was apprehensive, but found some solace knowing it was her last date with him. He answered the door, and invited her inside.

She wasn't dressed like a hooker. Conversely, she dressed conservatively, wearing a navy blue pleated skirt, long-sleeved white silk blouse and white heels. Her short dark hair, formed into a French twist. She was neatly groomed, and wore a minimum of makeup. She wore no undergarments, and looked more like a schoolgirl than a prostitute.

"Please have a seat," said Schmidt. "May I fix you a drink?"

"Water, please," said Monique.

Schmidt walked to his wet bar, removed two bottles of Evian natural spring water from his stainless steel mini refrigerator, poured them into crystal glasses and handed Monique hers on a small linen napkin.

"Thank you," said Monique.

"You're certainly welcome, Monique."

Monique was becoming increasingly nervous with each passing moment, especially with Schmidt's uncommon courtesy. She vividly recalled her last date when he bound her wrists and ankles to the four posts of his bed like an animal with nylon cord. He repeatedly had his way with her insisting she call him Heinrich while he called her Elsie. (Was that his mother's name?) He was a large man in many ways, and insisted she scream and moan during intercourse. Her screaming seemed to increase his animal passion. She loathed the experience, especially the foreign language (German) and his wearing of jackboots and the steel helmet. He threatened to tattoo her wrist with numbers, but relented when she panicked and swore to report him to the authorities. When he insisted she bite his member until it drew blood, she swore it would be her last visit to his home. Now here she was again. What we do for money, she thought.

This evening was different, so far. When they finished the Evian water, he insisted she join him in his Jacuzzi, and she did. It was an enjoyable experience. She began to feel at ease and let the forced jets of water relax her tense muscles. What the hell was going on? Monique was having a great time.

After the Jacuzzi, they dried off and went to bed where they had a truly enjoyable sexual relationship. Nothing kinky, just good hot sex. They climaxed together. It was Monique's first real orgasm in months.

Afterwards, Schmidt thanked her profusely, and, in addition to the regular fee, paid her an additional one hundred dollars, and wished her well. She was flabbergasted and called her chauffeur for a ride back to her apartment at the Jefferson Towers on the Detroit River.

Schmidt told Monique to wait in his home for her ride, as he had an appointment to keep. "Please lock the front door when you leave, dear," Schmidt asked pleasantly and kissed her on the cheek as he left the house.

Forty minutes later, Monique entered her suite at the Towers, an exclusive gated community—still in awe of her pleasant experience with Schmidt. Guess I was wrong about him, she thought.

She slipped out of her clothes, carefully hanging up the blue pleated skirt in the large walk-in closet filled with thousands of dollars worth of very expensive and appropriate clothes. A working girl must look good, she thought. She placed five one-hundred-dollar bills on her nightstand, and congratulated herself on another profitable evening. Holly let the girls keep tips. She thought, three hundred dollars profit—Holly gets two hundred. Not too shabby.

Stepping out of the shower, feeling good about the world, she sensed something amiss. She opened the bathroom door, and standing in front of her, wearing nothing but jackboots, a German steel helmet, an iron cross on a chain, dangling from an erection, and a belted holster around his waist was Schmidt.

Schmidt's P-38 was leveled at her chest. Monique crossed her arms in front of her small but pert breasts said, "Oh, Jesus," and started to scream.

Schmidt said two words, "Good-bye, Elsie," and opened fire emptying the clip of eight nine-mm hollow points—four into her chest, two into her forehead, and two into her mouth.

Schmidt dressed and collected the shell casings, eased into Monique's bedroom and picked up the five crisp one hundred dollar bills off her nightstand. She won't be needing this, he thought.

Fifty-Four

Holly received a call from the Detroit Police Department three days after Monique's decomposing body was found in her suite at the Jefferson Towers. An adjacent tenant complained of an offensive odor coming from Monique's suite and the manager opened her door to find her body. The police were called and an investigation began.

She had no known living relatives, but a note in her purse said to contact Holly in the event of an emergency.

Holly was shattered. Not only was Monique a most sought-after date, and terrific moneymaker, but also was as close a friend as Holly could have in the whoring business. Holly arranged and paid for the funeral, attendant costs and burial at White Chapel Cemetery in Troy, Michigan.

Monique would have turned thirty next month. Thirty years of age is rather old for a prostitute, Helen thought, but still too damn young to die.

Twenty girls, Holly and one man showed up at Monique's funeral. All the female attendees were employees of Holly's. She thought it ironic that the only man friend that showed up was Schmidt. The others, who had been so desperate to see Monique in life, gave a flip about her in death. She found it rather touching, but odd, that Kurt Schmidt would come to the funeral.

When Holly was first informed of Monique's murder, she had a feeling Schmidt was involved. He had threatened her and her kids—bastard kids, he called them, but would he stoop that low? She hoped not. Should she contact the police and tell them about her suspicions? Schmidt probably still had contacts with the Detroit P.D. Perhaps she should mind her own business and let the cops do their thing. Maybe they would find the killer—maybe not. Probably not in this terrible, vicious city.

Monique's 401-K fund reverted to Holly as there were no beneficiaries or dependents named. She divided the money up and gave her girls a bonus, compliments of Monique. Monique's clothes, after her suite was released as a crime scene, were given to and shared by the girls. Monique was buried in her blue pleated skirt and long sleeved white silk blouse—her favorite outfit.

Holly would have to advertise for a replacement for Monique. She made a mental note to run an ad in the Oakland Press. She hated the screening and interviewing process that followed. She normally rejected nine of ten applicants.

Fifty-Five

Black Lake is located in Cheboygan and Presque Isle counties in northern Michigan. It is Michigan's seventh largest inland lake and attracts tens of thousands of visitors annually with its natural beauty, boating, water-related sports, including many varieties of fish, sturgeons to yellow perch, bass, walleye, muskellunge and a few more.

The United Auto Workers has maintained the Walter and Mary Reuther educational center at Black Lake since the 1960s and each year host thousands of UAW members, active, retired, and family members.

The center's banquet hall seated and served well more than five hundred people, and was jammed to capacity on a cool Michigan September evening. Fifty-five tables, each seating ten, were attentively listening to the UAW chaplain saying grace, thanking Heavenly Father for all the gifts that had been bestowed on those present, and those unable to attend. The hall was silent except for an occasional cough or sneeze. Everyone was grateful, and thankful to be alive in such a tranquil setting, in the presence of family and friends.

As the chaplain said amen, a horrendous fireball followed by an ear-splitting white-hot explosion erupted in the center of the dining area. Fire spread quickly from the floor to the ceiling and walls. Those not incinerated were fatally burned. Many died of smoke inhalation. Some were cut to pieces by flying objects and broken shards of glass. Several were stomped and trampled to death by the few hysterical survivors in their frenzied rush to escape the inferno. The screams seem to have emanated from the deepest bowels of hell.

There was a total of sixty survivors of the nightmare on Black Lake. Many of them would undergo weeks of excruciatingly painful burn therapy. One beautiful young woman, a waitress, lost her ears, nose, lips and eye lids. They simply melted off.

The Cheboygan Memorial Hospital was simply not equipped to handle this high number of casualties. Patients were transported to medical facilities in

Roger's City, Petosky, Kinross Air Force Base, and as far away as Sault Ste. Marie, Michigan, in Michigan's upper peninsula.

By the time local fire departments arrived, the destruction was complete. The cement foundation was the only part of the structure not entirely ruined.

The next day's edition of the Cheboygan Sentinel had a one-word headline.

WHY?

Fifty-Six

The public relations staff at Mega Motors issued a national press release advising MM employees and retirees not to gather in groups of more than twenty-four.

Finally, MM acknowledged there may be an inherent threat and danger directed at employees and former employees of the corporation. MM was working tirelessly with authorities to help put an end to the threat or alleged threat. They attempted to assure all that the safety and well-being of the MM family were first and foremost.

Of course, MM overreacted as usual, issuing individual plant directives to managers and personnel directors banning meetings in which total attendance exceeded twenty people.

This directive included all company-sponsored outings, conventions, retirement parties, political gatherings, classroom activities, training sessions, etc.

A similar directive emerged from UAW headquarters to all local presidents and chairmen in the nation, but did not stipulate as to maximum "safe" numbers in groups. It simply stated to the members to be vigilant in light of recent killings.

J.D. was schedule to go to Black Lake, but at the last minute, changed his mind and cancelled the trip. He was very lucky, indeed. Had he gone, statistically, he would have been killed.

Eleanor, Ryan and J.D. read the MM press release and union directive on their respective lunch breaks. They were not impressed.

After lunch, Ryan called Eleanor, and said, "Hi El, what do you think about the PR department's latest and greatest?"

"Typical MM bullshit," said Eleanor.

"Sounds like they are just covering their ass," said Ryan.

"Exactly," stated Eleanor.

"You know, and J.D. nearly went to Black Lake where so many people were killed," Ryan mentioned.

"Yes," Eleanor said. "He called me earlier today and told me. He also said he had read MM's bullshit directive as well as the UAW's."

"What did he have to say about them?" asked Ryan.

"That, and I quote J.D., both were written by morons."

"He has a way with words," said Ryan.

"When am I going to see you again?" asked Ryan.

"Did you forget, we've been living together since your divorce became final?" said Eleanor.

"I meant what time this evening," said Ryan laughing.

"Same time. Around five thirty," said Eleanor.

"You want me to call J.D. and have him come over for a cookout?" asked Ryan.

"Sure," said Eleanor. "See you then. Oh, better buy beer for J.D. "

"Will do. Bye, El."

Fifty-Seven

Kurt Schmidt, in less than five years, had recruited three hundred of the most sadistic and vicious killers in the world. Many were sons, daughters and grandchildren and great-grandchildren of Nazis who had escaped war-ravaged Germany in the middle 1940s and, with new identities, lived and prospered in Brazil, Argentina, New York and Canada. They settled and chose to live quietly awaiting a reborn fuhrer to lead them into a new world order.

These fanatical recruits were dedicated to the same principles as his SS father, and, like Heinrich, swore allegiance to their new fuhrer, Kurt Schmidt.

They were not the ignorant brazen skinheads that stupidly marched in silly parades, carrying swastika flags, insulting Jews and blacks. Nor were they the oafish neo-Nazis, walking hand in hand with Klansmen, swearing allegiance to misunderstood doctrine.

Schmidt's SSS (Supreme Security Staff) members had each sworn blood oaths to Kurt Schmidt, and awaited his orders. They had each been home-schooled and trained since birth to believe they were the supermen and -women of tomorrow, and would one day reunite and follow their fuhrer to wherever he may lead them.

Schmidt's organizational chart was patterned after Hitler's SS. The training and armament of the elite SSS had taken years, but now, according to Schmidt's Reich fuhrer, Hans Burger, they were ready to do the work of their fuhrer.

The radical mid-eastern Muslims made Schmidt's plans much easier to implement. With America's law enforcement agencies concentrating so much effort and time on the radical towel-heads, the stealth training of his elite SSS had greatly accelerated.

With Schmidt having amassed considerable wealth from MM and dozens of millionaire supporters, sophisticated world-class weaponry, albeit mostly small arms and assault rifles, had been furnished to his fanatical killers.

They simply awaited orders from Kurt Schmidt, their fuhrer.

Fifty-Eight

After Eleanor, Ryan and J.D. finished eating a plate of hamburgers, Kogle hot dogs, and Better-made potato chips; they moved from his deck into Ryan's great room and discussed current events.

J.D., nursing his third Stroh's, said, "It seems strange."

"What do you mean, J.D.?" asked Ryan.

"Strange that MM issued their letter about keeping groups to a minimum of twenty," said J.D.

"Not so strange," said Eleanor. "They had to make some statement after all the deaths."

"Why now?" asked J.D. "Why not after the *Columbia*, the stadium, the banquet hall....?"

"Who knows?" said Ryan. "Maybe they're just slow. You know, they say MM is like a big battleship—difficult to change course."

"Not so slow when they decide to take away our benefits," said J.D.

"Well, J.D.," said Eleanor, "the changes in our benefits were probably planned ten years ago."

"So I hear," responded J.D.

"But I bet," said J.D., "they wouldn't be so damn slow reacting if one of their big shots was blown away. I guess I'm just bitter. I lost some good friends at Black Lake."

"We've all lost good friends," added Ryan.

"It just seems like everyone is dragging their knuckles in making arrests. Meanwhile, our brothers, sisters, and pals are being scorched. Something has to be done," said J.D.

Ryan's telephone rang.

"El," he said, "would you answer that?"

"Who is it?" asked Ryan.

"I can't believe it! It's David. He's back in town. He says he has a plan and is on his way here to discuss it with us."

"Where is he?" asked Ryan.

"In our driveway," said Eleanor, as the doorbell rang.

Seeing David Wentz was a terrific surprise. When he went back to Israel, J.D., Ryan and Eleanor thought, they would never see their friend again. Now, here he was in the flesh looking great—rested, confident and determined.

"David, it's so good to see you. Can I get you something to drink?" asked Eleanor.

"Water would be fine, thanks," said David.

"What brings you back to murder city?" asked J.D.

"I'm here on assignment again, only this time at the behest of the Mossad and your government," answered David.

"Uh," said J.D., "you aren't supposed to be telling us any of this, are you?"

"No, of course not," said David, "but unseen by any of you, you've all been scanned for honesty and integrity by a tiny Dick Tracy sensor concealed in my watch pocket. Lucky for all of you it detected no skullduggery."

When they stopped laughing, Ryan said, "David, you are acting more like a crazy American every day."

"I consider that a great compliment," said David.

"I can't go into any detail, of course, but can tell you certain elements of your government and mine have infiltrated a very subversive organization felt to be controlled by a certain individual of Germanic origin," said David.

"Schmidt?" asked Eleanor.

"I'm sorry, I really can't say anymore," said David.

"Ve half vaze of making you talk," joked J.D.

When they quit laughing, David said, "You'll find out soon enough."

Fifty-Nine

Clark asked Schmidt to report to his office to discuss legacy reduction. Again, Schmidt strode by Eleanor as if she didn't exist and walked directly into Clark's office.

"Mr. Clark," began Schmidt, "I am pleased to announce the beginning of the latest phase of down-sourcing."

"I'd rather you refer to it as legacy reduction," said Clark, his tongue rapidly darting back and forth.

Schmidt thought, how dare you question my vocabulary, you tongue-darting lizard, but went on as though he heard and saw nothing.

"Now that I've been furnished a complete list of MM retirees, by address and telephone number, the process of elimination will begin in earnest."

"What do you mean, in earnest?" asked a testy, tongue-darting Clark.

"What I mean," said Schmidt, "is exactly what I said."

"Be more specific," urged Clark.

"Specifically," said Schmidt, "twenty-two MM retirees per day will be liquidated throughout the country. Their names will be chosen at random. Would you like for me to go into detail as to the methods of extermination?"

Clark, observing a seething rage emanating from Schmidt's facial expressions and hand gestures, said, "That sounds like a good even number. I needn't know any additional detail."

Schmidt excused himself from Clark's office and returned to his own. As soon as he sat down, he turned his computer on, and sent a short e-mail to his staff:

Legacy Blitz

Within three days after Schmidt's orders, throughout various parts of the country, MM retirees simply started dying. The majority of the killings were accomplished with handguns, but some died of knife wounds, beatings, burnings, drowning, and in a few cases, poisoning. In such a huge country, and in such random locations, it was practically impossible to detect any kind of pattern. Schmidt knew his SSS troops would be efficient and deadly. Each, as part of their blood oath to Schmidt, was prepared to die should authorities ever capture them. Death squads of three gave daily progress reports to their squad leader, who monitored their activities closely, and in turn reported to his superior, and so forth.

After several weeks, Metropolitan Life Insurance Company became alarmed at the significant increase in death insurance claims being filed by MM retiree beneficiaries.

A call was made from Metropolitan Life in New York to MM's Detroit Regional Personnel Center advising them of a dramatic increase in death claims, but initially an assistant manager in Detroit viewed it as merely an aberration.

After another month, a senior Metropolitan manager, Frank James, called Jim Burton, the manager of Detroit MM Regional Personnel with some disturbing facts. The average number of MM retiree death benefit claims for the past four years was one hundred and fifteen per month. This figure was constant, according to Metropolitan, peaking somewhat around the Christmas holidays. In the past thirty days, seven hundred and seventy-five death benefits claims were made—more than six times the average.

Metropolitan would have to increase their staff to process these claims in a timely manner, said the Metro manager.

"So, increase your staff," said the surly MM personnel manager. "It's not really my concern. We've paid premiums for these insurance policies and have no control over when people are going to die."

"What I'm saying," said James, "is that we deal with statistics and actuarial tables. What's happening is surely more than an aberration, and while I'm certainly not telling you what to do, Jim, I am saying something is happening to your retirees that should not be happening."

"Thanks for the information, Frank. Good-bye," said Burton.

Burton then felt he should cover his bottom side, and placed a call to his boss, the vice-president of personnel operations, Linda Duncan, who was out of town on company business. He left a message for the VP to contact him upon her return.

In three days, Ms. Duncan returned Burton's call. When the manager told her of the call from Metro, and the drastic increase in retiree death claims, the VP immediately said, "Jim, don't bother me with such trivial matters."

Ms. Duncan, in a typical MM shuffle, placed two calls, the second to Kurt Schmidt, chief of MM security. The call was immediately taken by Liz Lange and forwarded to Schmidt.

"Schmidt, this is Linda Duncan. It seems like many of our retirees are dying off—many more than normal. I don't think it's a big deal—but you might want to nose around and see what the hell's happening."

Schmidt, infuriated by the call, said, "Ms. Duncan, my role as head of MM's security precludes involvement in issues concerning retirees."

Duncan, incensed by Schmidt's attitude, retorted, "Schmidt, I've already spoken with your boss, Mr. Clark, and he concurs with my suggestion. You will investigate the inordinate number of retiree deaths. Is that clear?"

"Yes, Ms. Duncan. Right away." Schmidt thought, you are talking down to me, bitch, as though I need sensitivity training. If you only knew. And what the hell is wrong with Clark? He should stick to counting beans. The tongue-poking dunce.

Schmidt immediately called Clark's office and demanded to see Clark at his earliest convenience. Eleanor put Schmidt on hold and checked with her boss, who told Eleanor to send him in.

"Mr. Clark," an angry Schmidt said, "Can you explain why Ms. Duncan is telling me what to do? I thought I reported to you, only. "

"Well," a shaky Clark said, "I had to tell her something, Schmidt."

"Why didn't you tell her to piss up a rope?" asked Schmidt. "You know what's happening, for Christ's sake."

Before Clark could answer, Schmidt said, "And also, let's clear the air once and for all."

I have in my possession a recording, in which you clearly stated, "Schmidt is expendable.

"Would you like to explain that to me—now?"

Clark, clearly taken aback, said, "Schmidt, I have no earthly idea what you are talking about. Why would I ever say something so ludicrous?"

"I have no idea," said Schmidt, "But it's obviously your voice. It's a threat, and I do not take threats lightly."

Clark was now stammering, tongue poking and perspiring profusely. "Schmidt, think about it. One, I have no motive to have you removed. Two, I have no means in which to do so. Three, I respect you for your ability to get things done, and four, I need you. I fear someone has attempted to cause ill feelings between us, and it appears they have succeeded."

"Tell me Clark," asked Schmidt, "do you swear on the lives of your children—no wait—do you swear on your life you did not utter those three words—Schmidt is expendable?"

Clark, thinking fast said, "Kurt, I swear by all that is holy and on my life and lives of my children that, while those words may have come out of my mouth, they, in no way, came out in the order in which you heard them."

Schmidt thought for a moment, then said, "Mr. Clark, I believe you. Someone has attempted to drive a wedge between us, and, unfortunately, it nearly worked. Who has access to your office?"

Clark, greatly relieved, said, "Well, just Eleanor and the janitor, and of course, individuals I've asked to see. I don't suspect my secretary or the janitor."

"Perhaps you are too trusting, Mr. Clark. Fortunately, I'm not," Schmidt said, leaving Clark's office. Schmidt looked at Eleanor with contempt as he hurriedly walked by her desk.

When Schmidt returned to his office, he viewed with pride a top-secret document outlining his command structure.

Kurt Schmidt ************** Fuhrer
Hans Burger ************** Reich fuhrer
Eight ************** Obergruppenfuhrer
Twenty ************** Kommandoamt
270 ************** SSS Shock Troopers

Two hundred seventy SSS troopers were grouped in threes. The ninety subgroups were located in geographical areas throughout the United States where the greatest concentrations of MM retirees were located.

Twenty Kommandoamts supervised between thirteen and fourteen troopers.

Kommandoamts reported to their respective eight regional Obergruppenfuhrer.

Obergruppenfuhrer answered directly to Hans Burger, the Reichfuhrer.

The organization was Schmidt's replication of the original layout of Heinrich Himmler's organizational structure when Himmler was Reichfuhrer and chief of the German Police.

Hans Burger was Schmidt's right-hand man and chief confidante. Burger was his eyes and ears—a true Aryian—Schmidt's Himmler.

Sixty

Hans Burger was a child of the nineteen-forties. His parents fled war-torn Germany when Hans was six years old. They purchased a small white frame home on Studebaker Street in what was then Van Dyke, Michigan. The front of their home faced Lincoln Elementary School, which was located directly across the street. Hans enrolled in September of nineteen-forty-four as a first grader.

He knew little English, but was a fast learner. Initially, his schoolmates were very kind, but by the third grade, several classmates began to make fun of his German accent.

One evening, Hans overheard his father cursing loudly as he walked into their home. Hans couldn't understand why his usually patient and quiet father was so upset.

Hans walked out onto their front porch and suddenly realized why his papa had become so incensed. A large black swastika had been hastily painted with a wide brush on the front of their entrance door. Although Hans was just eight years of age, he knew the swastika represented German evil. Now, to his utter dismay, he felt the entire neighborhood viewed him and his parents as the Nazi enemy.

Mr. Burger quickly obtained a quart of white house paint and repainted the front door, but the damage had been done. Although Hans and his parents were technically US citizens, they never felt as foreign as now. Hans thought he could never be a real American, and the thought was devastating.

Hans wondered. What is a real American? He discovered most of the neighborhood kids were not born in Michigan. Many were hillbillies from Kentucky, Tennessee, and West Virginia. Other kids had parents and grandparents from Poland, the Ukraine, Italy, Finland, and a boy from Greece. Why was Hans different? He was a square head and kraut.

By the time Hans entered junior high school (now called middle school) he adapted to having few friends and a sparse social life. Hans was a handsome, well-built young man with a full head of dark wavy hair, buckeye brown eyes, and straight white teeth. He's never had a toothache or cavity. That was just as well as his father had no dental insurance and little money to spend on anything but the necessities of living.

Hans' father, Max Burger, was an engine mechanic, a trade he had learned in Germany. Mr. Burger worked in the garage at a local Chevrolet dealership as an automobile mechanic. He made little money, but the job was steady.

Mrs. Burger was a housewife, but two days a week, performed housekeeping and cleaning services for a widower, Mr. Wilson, who lived several blocks north on Maxwell Street. She cooked Mr. Wilson several meals each week and was paid ten dollars per day. She was thrilled to get the money. Some holidays, Mr. Wilson would surprise her with a one-dollar bonus. With this extra money, she would often purchase material, needles and thread from Stanley's five and dime store on Van Dyke Avenue, a few minutes' walk from their Studebaker home.

The Burgers spoke little English in the home, which may have accounted for Hans having a noticeable accent, which did little to endear him to children his age and many adults as well. Hans could have cared less. He could not forget the swastika incident.

When Hans entered Lincoln High School, he was still quite the loner. One afternoon, between classes, he bent over to get a drink of water at one of the hallway drinking fountains. From out of nowhere, the high school's star football jock purposely plowed into Hans with lowered shoulders knocking him down on the hard tiled floor.

Hans had never felt such pain, and wondered, while still on the floor, what the hell happened.

"You all right, Kraut?" asked grinning jock.

"Yeah," responded Hans.

"Next time," said the jock, "watch where the hell you're going."

Before Hans replied again, he noticed a tall, gangly skinny boy with a big nose and brown hair standing several feet away.

Big nose said, "Piss off, jock—you should watch where the hell you are going. Asshole!"

As soon as big nose said that, he took off running like a bat out of hell, with jock not far behind. In less than fifty feet, jock caught big nose, slammed him against a gray metal hallway locker, and drew back his ham hock fist to blast big nose in the nose.

Big nose closed his eyes in anticipation of the blow.

Fortunately, a teacher had observed the events and intervened mere seconds before jock struck big nose.

After school that afternoon, Hans saw big nose on the sidewalk in front of the high school, lighting up a Lucky Strike.

"Hey, thanks for what you did today. My name's Hans Burger. What's yours?"

"No problem, Burger. My name's Schmidt, Kurt Schmidt. Pleased to meet you."

Hans Burger and Kurt Schmidt became the closest of friends. They became allies when discovering their past and present situations were nearly identical. They were both born in Germany, had been shunned and embarrassed by classmates and neighbors alike.

One day they would be recognized for their true Aryan superiority.

Sixty-One

After supper, Ryan and Eleanor went for a walk in the local city park. It was a warm evening with a light southwesterly breeze puffing into their faces. The sun was setting and golden rays were darting through huge maple leaves, branches waving in hushed applause.

Ryan took Eleanor's hands and they stopped walking and stared into one another's eyes. He had never seen eyes as gorgeous as hers, a deep indigo, and a face as pure and innocent as when they first met. He was fourteen, she thirteen. Words can't begin to describe the chemistry that percolated between them. Now, half a life later, a miserable marriage and untold heartache they stood—inches apart, together, as one.

"I love you, El. I've loved you since the first time we met," spoke Ryan softly. "You are my reason for living."

"Ryan, I feel the same. I love you and have forever," spoke Eleanor. "We were meant to be together, forever."

Even though they had both been around the block a few times, the trust, admiration, and respect they felt for one another were as real as the sunset—as fresh as country morning dew.

For a brief moment in time, they could forget about their jobs, the past and the future. For this evening was theirs to be tender with each another—to express appreciation for the miracle of their love. They knew God had truly smiled upon them.

Their lovemaking was initially slow and rhythmic—each tenderly exploring the softness, hardness, dampness and desires of each other. As the intensity of need increased, so did the tempo of thrust, withdrawal, thrust—finally culminating into mutual moans of orgasmic ecstasy. They were as one, as it was meant to be.

After showering, Ryan and Eleanor slept a deep sleep sprinkled with dreams normally reserved for prepubescent children. Happy dreams. Sweet visions. Hugging dreams.

Their separate detours had finally converged into one narrow glorious path, upon which they now stood, hand in hand, together at last.

With everything going so well between Ryan and Eleanor, it was incredulous to everyone, except other alcoholics, that Ryan went on a wild drunken binge the very next day. So many things were finally going right in his life. He'd gotten a nice merit increase at work and was finally given his own office, complete with a door that actually locked—no more cubicles with fish bowl openness. He'd even been re-titled Benefit Coordinator, in charge of the benefit section.

After his week-long demon-ridden binge, Ryan returned home to an empty house. He'd taken the week off, but he still had three weeks of vacation time remaining. Eleanor emptied the house of her few belongings. She left Ryan a short note:

> Ryan,
>
> Call me when you have decided to quit drinking—not before.
>
> As ever,
> El

He wadded the note up, threw it on the floor, and staggered to the cupboard to have just a taste of vodka. He hated vodka, but hated himself even more, and needed something to calm his jittery nerves and screaming conscience. He was horrified to discover the alcohol had little sedative effect—actually. It made him felt worse. So he drank more—and more and more.

After the fifth of vodka was gone, Ryan literally felt himself dying—the pain in the area where he supposed his overworked liver resided was severe, but paled in intensity compared to the raging evil nightmare within his head.

Had Ryan not called John Stafford—MM Warren's substance abuse coordinator, Ryan surely would have died. When John answered Ryan's desperate phone call, John merely said, "I've been waiting for your call." John had seen Ryan slipping into the abyss of alcoholism even before Ryan recognized the symptoms. John drove to Ryan's house and personally drove him to a hospital known to have a good detox and rehabilitation unit.

Ryan had passed out, actually gone into an alcohol-induced coma, just prior to John loading him into his car. Subsequent blood tests revealed Ryan's blood alcohol content was 0.48. Zero point five zero usually resulted in death. Liver enzyme tests scored a new hospital high. The emergency room doctors nearly lost him.

The following day, when Ryan awoke, by his bedside was Eleanor and John. Ryan was alive and in the company of the two most important people in his life—the woman he loved and the man who saved his life.

When Ryan attempted to thank John for coming to his rescue, John downplayed his role and took no credit whatsoever. Instead, he said, "You would have done the same for me had our roles been reversed. Besides, I'm benefitting from your condition."

It took Ryan several months to understand how a drunk could help another drunk.

Strange—about the lives of drunks. At one time, John and Ryan were journeymen practicing alcoholics. Many a morning, when they were supervisors at MM, they would compare hangovers, and laugh at their foolishness, only to repeat their same self-destruction. Then, John decided to become a giver rather than a taker and dedicated his life to helping himself by helping others with their addiction to alcohol.

John Stafford met the love of his life, Dawn Colwell, shortly before his early retirement from MM. Dawn and John married after a short, but wonderfully exciting engagement, and moved into a lovely home facing Lake Huron near the small town of Port Sanilac, Michigan. John said, after the wedding, "Life is full of rewards and I married mine."

Sixty-Two

David Wentz headed a task force of forty-eight highly trained and very skilled United States/Israeli terrorist elimination experts. The TEE squad was formed after 9/11 and was a brainchild of the former secretary of defense, Adam Fairchild, and Saul Goldberg, then chief of Israel's Mossad.

Members of TEE operate independent of any known US military agency, and the government responsible for their creation denies their very existence.

Their mission is to seek and destroy known terrorists within the borders of the United States, or wherever they were required. They follow no rules of war, and take no prisoners. TEE members have complete authority to kill at will and their motives are not questioned.

TEE is, in fact, a bonafide death squad born out of desperation in the ensuing struggle against foreign and domestic terrorists. Legal? Absolutely not. Effective? Very.

David was aware of Schmidt's SSS killers, and the fact they were targeting MM retirees.

Ryan had been able to procure a list for David showing last month's beneficiary death claims including the decedent's former residence, etc. With that information, it was easy enough to determine where SSS killers had been and, in all likelihood, where they would continue to strike.

David has assumed Schmidt's SSS would strike randomly, but found retirees chose to live in particular parts of the country, such as Florida, Arizona, and generally settled within a one hundred-mile radius of where they spent so many years working.

He thought, I could use a TEE force of five hundred, but have to settle for what I have. David took a calculated risk and assigned all forty-eight TEES to the area most populated by MM retirees—Rochester, Michigan. Rochester, in Oakland Country, is around twenty miles north of Detroit, and fifteen miles south of Pontiac, Michigan.

The risk proved to be worth taking as four SSS members were shot to death by TEE the first night of the strike, and six killed the second. TEE ten, SSS zero.

Hans Burger placed a call to Schmidt at Schmidt's home. "Mein Fuhrer, we have lost ten SSS men in the past two nights. Unfortunately, our quota of forty-four in the same period was not met."

Schmidt calmly replied, "Reichfuhrer Burger, I have full confidence in your ability to pick up the slack. Guten Abend."

"Guten Abend, Mein Fuhrer," said Burger.

The SSS was able to pick up the pace. Daily murders in and around Rochester, and Oakland county increased within two weeks and the national average retiree death per day was again twenty-two. In addition, one TEE expert was killed in an exchange of gunfire and one more critically injured. TEE ten. SSS one.

The general public remained totally unaware of the violence occurring throughout the country. The media focused on natural disasters, tsunamis, hurricanes, tornadoes, famine, starving children, the price of milk and the state of the economy. One idiotic congressman suggested a moat be built adjacently to the wall between Mexico and several southern states to prevent illegal aliens from entering the country. There were rumors that Arizona residents were contemplating filling the moat with alligators and piranha.

David was dissatisfied with the lack of TEE's progress. At times he wondered if the plan to fight the force of evil with, what many would consider a like force of evil, would accomplish the ultimate goal of eliminating Schmidt's SSS.

He gave more and more consideration to removing the head of the serpent. Of course, that would be out and out murder. But, he thought, is eliminating a murderer evil? Hadn't Hitler's own generals attempted to kill him when they realized what a maniac he had become?

The number of murdered MM retirees was now in the thousands, and the carnage had begun only eight months ago. The annual number of homicides in the US, in this year alone, had increased from nineteen thousand in the previous year to more than twenty-five thousand—the highest number of domestic homicides in the history of the country, and the year was not yet over.

What happened the very next week made David's decision easy. It was necessary, logical, and too late in coming.

Eleanor arrived at work Wednesday. Another Hump Day, she thought. Another day of sobriety for Ryan. Thank God and AA. She told Ryan she would consider resuming their relationship after he remained sober for one year. She knew ultimatums didn't work but was ready to try anything, including Alanon. She felt she understood alcoholism as well as any non-alcoholic could. Hell, she knew alcoholics didn't thoroughly understand their own disease. She loved Ryan, and always would, but was determined to not enable his dependancy. She prayed for his recovery every morning and night.

Shortly before lunch, she received a Fed-Ex delivery in her office. After signing for the package, she read the attached card which simply stated, "Remember Me?" She suspected Ryan had sent her a gift. But what the heck could it be? It was a fairly large box—a gift-wrapped container around the size of a square basketball. Oh, he shouldn't have, she thought as she happily tore into the gift.

As she cut through the cellophane wrapping tape that sealed the item, she smelled something rather odd. Could it be food that spoiled? She carefully turned the box upside down. Whatever it was, weighed at least ten or twelve pounds. After lifting the box up, exposing the contents, she froze, screamed and immediately collapsed. J.D.'s head wobbled to and fro on the plexiglass cover of her desk for a few seconds before resting on its ghastly decaying side.

Eleanor's next moment of clarity occurred in the emergency room of Henry Ford hospital. She was in shock, hoping beyond hope, believing beyond belief she had awoken from a horrible dream. She was given a sedative and discharged from the hospital that evening with a prescription for Ativan, ten mg—no refills.

Clark heard Eleanor's scream and walked into her office—saw her unconscious on the floor, then saw J.D.'s head. He retched violently, but composed himself long enough to call in-house security who responded within seconds. The security officer called 911, and paramedics, along with the Detroit police responded within five minutes.

Eleanor was placed on a stretcher after paramedics checked her vitals, finding her relatively stable, she was then transported to Henry Ford Hospital—a few short blocks away from MM headquarters.

Police officers secured the scene and contacted homicide detectives who thoroughly investigated the location, took pictures, checked the box and wrappings for prints, and finally removed the head from Eleanor's desktop.

Clark became violently ill, barely able to make it to his bathroom before vomiting repeatedly.

Security contacted the local union and asked them to send janitors to Clark and Eleanor's offices for thorough cleaning. The union man advised security that the janitors would have to be paid time and one half, as it would exceed their normal eight-hour shifts.

Sixty-Three

J.D. was buried at Cadillac Memorial East Gardens in Clinton Township, Michigan. His torso had been located in a dumpster on Detroit's east side. The funeral was attended by hundreds of UAW brothers and sisters. David, Ryan and Eleanor were there, although Eleanor was still recovering from the horror of the incident.

Not one single big shot from the Building bothered paying their respects. While their absence from the services was predictable, it was still shameless.

J.D. had no family, other than his UAW brothers and sisters. Surprisingly, his last will and testament left all his worldly goods, and considerable cash, including several acres of land in Lapeer county, to Eleanor, who was also named beneficiary to his quarter-million-dollar life insurance policy.

J.D., who had been full of mirth and surprises in life had inserted an addendum to his will that said:

> To those who question why I chose to leave it all to Eleanor, I did so because she's one cool chick.
>
> J.D.

Classic J.D. "There will never be another one like him," said a tearful Eleanor.

David and Ryan concurred.

Eleanor went on a sick leave of absence as recommended by her treating psychiatrist. Her doctor indicated she would be off work a minimum of eight to ten weeks. She was prescribed antidepressants and a nightly sedative for sleep. Although it hadn't been a year since Ryan quit drinking, she relented on her ultimatum and asked if she could move back in with him. He was overjoyed.

Ryan thought, not many saps like me get another chance after screwing up so badly. Dear God, please let me live the right kind of life—the good life. He prayed to God that he would be spared the evil attraction of alcohol. He prayed every morning and every evening before he slept, thanking God for the day, asking God to bless his loved ones.

Eleanor asked Ryan's opinion about her quitting her job at MM. She felt she could never go back to work for Clark. The horrible memories of J.D. haunted her both day and night.

Ryan felt she should not resign, but stay on sick leave. If she didn't fully recuperate, to think about a long-term sick leave, or perhaps an early retirement. She agreed to follow Ryan and her doctor's advice.

Ryan benefitted from Eleanor's presence in his house. She being there took his mind off himself and his demons. For the first time in a long time, his thoughts and deeds helped someone, and someone he loved more than himself. He started including Eleanor in his morning and evening prayers, praying for both of them to grow in the strength of God's blessings. And they most certainly did.

Sixty-Four

David had no doubt who killed or ordered the killing of J.D. The beheading of J.D. and subsequent display to Eleanor was a heinously sadistic terror tactic meant to horrify and frighten others into submission—to send souls cowering and pleading for mercy. While Eleanor was indeed frightened, suffering from anxiety neurosis, David was furious and more determined than ever. His rage accelerated into hatred. He would remove the head of the evil serpent, the would-be Fuhrer, the murdering assassin—Kurt Schmidt. And, he would relish the task.

Schmidt had indeed supervised the kidnaping and malicious beheading of J.D. and personally witnessed his horrible death. The thrashing and gurgling of J.D. as the serrated knife sawed through his throat, tendons and cervical column brought a thrill to Schmidt he hadn't felt since killing Monique or was her name Elsie… he wondered. No, no, it was Monique, Holly's slut.

Although Schmidt was in his early sixties, he was strong and fit. He ate well, exercised regularly and had frequent medical examinations. He took no medications. His blood pressure, pulse, and general health was that of a thirty-year-old. His mental health was another matter.

Schmidt made a decision and directed Reich Fuhrer Burger to implement it immediately. The SSS was to be withdrawn from Oakland County, Michigan, and scattered throughout the nation. The goal of twenty-two dead MM retirees per day was unchanged. Schmidt was unhappy losing ten crack SSS troopers in Michigan and felt redeployment was necessary to elude further detection and elimination.

The random elimination of retirees was next to impossible to predict or prevent. David's decision to personally kill Schmidt was discussed with his most trusted staff. He told six of his confidantes of his plan to exterminate Schmidt. They agreed that this bold move was necessary, but fraught with danger. The killer—David Wentz—would most certainly be captured if not killed himself. Schmidt was surrounded by highly trained SSS guards at this point and was rarely seen. He had taken a fully paid extended leave of absence from his job as MM's head of security—all with the blessing of Sheldon Clark.

Still, David was determined. He met with Ryan and Eleanor to make them aware of the planned assassination. He was pleasantly surprised to see Eleanor in reasonably good health and Ryan happier that he'd ever seen him.

Eleanor had taken an early retirement and Ryan had been transferred to MM's regional personnel center in Detroit—near the MM Building. Ryan suspected the consolidation of MM's personnel operations would eventually result in the elimination of his, and other personnel functions, but decided to take each day at a time. He was nearing his thirty-year mark in service and soon would be able to retire. Ryan's multi-tasked job in benefits had changed considerably and now only handled non-litigated workers' compensation claims for ten MM plants in Michigan.

When David apprised Eleanor and Ryan of his intention to kill Schmidt, they were not surprised, but were concerned for his safety. David went on to tell his friends he had decided Schmidt would probably never allow himself to be brought to trial, and it was perfectly ethical, at least in Israel, to kill enemies who could be not brought to trial.

Eleanor said, "Isn't that stretching logic a tiny bit?"

David merely shrugged his shoulders, smiled, and said, "Not in Israel, Eleanor."

Eleanor started to say something to the effect that they were in Michigan, USA, but knew nothing would stop David from doing what he felt was necessary.

David tried to assure them it was just another necessary hit. He had not fully developed strategy for Schmidt's killing. It might take a month or longer. David said, "I'm going dark, so you will not see me or have any communication with me until it's over, if then. The number I'll leave is only to be used in case of the most imminent danger. I seldom tell civilians of my plans, but you, Ryan and Eleanor, have become my best friends in America—perhaps my only friends. I've come to love you like sister and brother. Should I fail in this endeavor, rest assured, I will have given it my very best."

David hugged Eleanor, then David, and said a tearful goodbye.

Eleanor said, "I wish I'd told him about our wedding plans, Ryan. Perhaps, we will when his mission has been accomplished."

"I'll ask him to be my best man," replied Ryan. "The wedding is not for another month. Let's hope he'll be available."

"Let's hope," said Eleanor

Sixty-Five

Ryan received an alarming call one morning while working at the personnel center. It was from, what sounded like, a young woman in much distress. She identified herself as a Mrs. Amy Horton, and wondered if she was entitled to any benefits as her husband, Steve Horton, had been killed while at work.

Ryan scheduled a meeting the very next morning with Mrs. Horton. Investigation revealed Mr. Horton, recently discharged from the US Marines, had obtained a job as a plant security guard at the old MM chassis plant in Livonia, Michigan.

Steve Horton was making his routine plant rounds at one thirty A.M. (he worked the graveyard shift) and noticed a door, slightly ajar, at the rear of the huge stamping plant that manufactured bumpers, coil and leaf springs. The door was supposed to have been locked.

As Steve investigated further, one, or perhaps more than one individual, took him by surprise. There was a struggle, and Steve had been shot in the back of the head with a small-caliber handgun. His lifeless body was discovered shortly thereafter by another security guard who had been unable to contact him via radio. He was pronounced dead on arrival at St. Mary's hospital in Livonia.

The ensuing police investigation was unable to determine who was responsible for Steve Horton's untimely death. Perhaps, he had come across an illicit drug transaction.

Ryan was no stranger to death benefits. He had handled many, but this was the first murder involving worker's compensation benefits. He felt great empathy for Amy Horton. At their meeting, she still exhibited understandable grief, anger and despair.

Ryan processed her claim immediately and tried to express his deepest sympathy to her. She met her husband when they were in the Marines. She did not look like a Marine, Ryan thought. Sadly, Amy Horton told Ryan that

Steve had recently given his two-week notice as he had obtained a much better job elsewhere.

Amy Horton's five hundred weeks of compensation was not much as her husband made the minimum payable, as he was newly hired. His average weekly wage—used to calculate compensation benefits was so small, Ryan issued checks payable based on the maximum allowable in cases where the actual earnings were so small.

Ryan thought of the thousands of other deaths in which the same feelings of angst, bitterness, and total grief were thrust upon untold numbers of innocent spouses and loved ones. It was incomprehensible that anyone could knowingly be responsible for such horror and dread. Death, at its most optimal time, is never without heartache and tears. Perhaps Schmidt's demise would be viewed differently, thought Ryan.

Sixty-Six

Eleanor occupied her time with wedding plans. Both she and Ryan had outgrown the needs for a huge wedding and reception. They planned on a simple civil ceremony and would have dinner at the Van Dyke Club in Detroit. Eleanor would wear a plain white dress. Ryan planned on wearing a simple black suit, shirt and tie. All the preliminary legal requirements had been handled. The honeymoon would be a romantic weekend at an exclusive resort hotel in Traverse City, Michigan, overlooking Grand Traverse Bay.

They had both overcome major obstacles in life. Eleanor, a few sordid affairs, and Ryan, a divorce, alcoholism, and more affairs than he cared to remember. Both had suffered the loss of dear friends. Ryan's alcoholism was an ongoing daily challenge, but much easier with Eleanor at his side. They hoped for a bit of the happiness they saw and felt each time they thought of John and Dawn Stafford.

But the thing that weighed most heavily on their minds was the ongoing butchery of MM retirees by Schmidt, Clark and their band of murdering devils. Eleanor thought, gosh a retiree is not at all safe—then she thought—Hell, I'm a retiree now!

Ryan convinced Eleanor into taking an eight-hour handgun safety class with him to obtain a concealed weapon's permit. The class, quite interesting and fun, culminated in each shooting a silhouette of a person forty-eight times at varying distances in an indoor gun range. Surprisingly, Eleanor scored considerably higher than Ryan, who considered himself a great white hunter. All required after the class was the payment of the fee, a fingerprint scanning, a mug shot, and await the issuance of the permit.

When the permits came (Eleanor's arrived one week before Ryan's), Ryan thought his mug shot was of some crazed convicted felon—a demented soul, perhaps, but it was a good likeness, according to Eleanor. Eleanor complained her photo made her look fat, but Ryan thought it was beautiful.

Both prayed they would never have to use their handgun. Ryan had a Smith and Wesson 357mag. Model 686 and Eleanor owned a Smith and Wesson 38 Special. They practiced once a week at the same range they took their safety class. They each remembered one key thing taught in the safety class. You are responsible for each shot fired.

Eleanor had an occasional nightmare in which J.D.'s bloody head rolled out of a box on her night stand, bobbled a while, then stared and finally spoke to her, saying, "Help me!"

She would awaken soaked with sweat—screaming for Ryan who was quick to try and console her. The horrible dream occurred less often, but with the same graphic torturous gripping fear as the first time she dreamed it. Sometimes, she felt she was losing it, and might have had it not been for Ryan's strength and patience. They needed each another more and more with each tick of the clock.

David never bothered telling Eleanor or Ryan, but he had assigned two of the best Tee members available providing round the clock protection for his American friends. These two men would sacrifice themselves to protect Eleanor and Ryan. They were the best of the best.

Sixty-Seven

Calviston "Crutch Tip" Jamison was assigned the office janitor job opening at the MM building to replace J.D. Crutch Tip was named accordingly after part of his left foot was amputated after being mangled in an industrial accident. The unspoken truth was, when Calveston worked at the old MM Axle plant, he didn't believe the fork lift trucks were as heavy as stated in bold print on both sides of the six- to eight-ton battery-powered vehicles. To prove his point, he placed his left foot under the right rear solid rubber tire and dared the operator to back over it. The truck driver took the dare flattening Calviston's foot to pancake size resulting in the subsequent partial amputation of the left foot.

When Calviston returned to work, he was on crutches, and tagged "Crutch Tip" accordingly. He liked the name and it stuck. Had he disliked the name, it would have stuck. It was better than Shit on a stick—a nickname given to a friend of Claviston, who had suffered a partial amputation of the right leg—up to the knee, in an industrial accident. Shit on a stick was named appropriately, as he was an unusual whiny, non-productive, sorry member of the work force. Calviston could not even remember Shit on a stick's real name.

Crutch Tip liked his new assignment on the executive floor of the MM building cleaning offices and bathrooms of the corporation's big shots. He wasn't smart enough to do anything with the tooth brushes like his predecessor, J.D. Crutch Tip did the bare minimum as was his nature. Seniority had certain privileges and the old Crutch took advantage of them. He knew the executives were mostly spoiled rich dudes afraid to say anything to the rank and file, so they could just piss off.

So, Crutch sang, whistled and hummed during his shift—which was the afternoon shift—from three thirty P.M. until midnight. Usually by five o'clock the big wigs were gone leaving him alone to sing songs he had composed in his small head. His favorite was "Rat Face Reggie." The song had a Reggae beat. He would sing a few bars while leaning on his left arm crutch pushing a small vacuum with his right hand and arm.

Rat face Reggie had a hell of a roll
Kept it with his keys and chain
Loved Tamika with half his soul
The other half loved cocaine
Had alligator shoes and a white mink hat
Skinny as a snake, nimble as a cat
Man that dude was slick as ice
Cocaine cool and high

Crutch Tip danced—as well as a cripple could—and had a wonderful time working for the man. He had graduated to one crutch, but could have gotten by with a cane. He felt a crutch was more in keeping with his new name.

Calviston, being a cripple, favored his good right leg and foot. He soon noticed his right shoe—sole and heel, was wearing while his left shoe remained as new. Because this injury was compensable under the Michigan workers' compensation statute, the company bought him a new pair of shoes whenever he requested them.

The workers' compensation benefit representative, seeing that one shoe was being replaced, practically unworn, called Calviston and asked him if he would consider wearing the unworn left shoe on the right foot, thus saving the company money.

Calviston told the rookie representative the only place the shoe would fit would be up his ass, and he never heard from the workers' compensation representative again.

Crutch tried to convince his wife, Jasmine, he was an office manager at the Building, and she half-believed and half didn't care, so long as he worked, stayed out of her face and brought home some money.

Occasionally, when his stub of a foot ached, he would sit on Clark's toilet—sometimes on Clark's chair and compose more music. He dreamed of the day when his music would make him famous and rich. Could happen, he hoped.

One evening, Crutch got drunk on his lunch break—drank a bottle of Wild Irish Rose—returned to Clark's office, staggered into the bath, curled into a ball in the corner, passed out and dreamed of being an acclaimed blues artist.

Upon Clark's arrival to work the following morning, he walked into his personal bath to see a disheveled black man passed out on the bathroom floor with a crutch lying adjacent to his body. Clark screamed like a little girl awakening Crutch. His screams also brought several security guards scrambling to the scene.

Crutch gathered his wits quickly and told Mr. Clark he must have passed out from his diabetes and high blood. Clark bought into the scam, offered to call 911, but Crutch thanked him, saying he was fine now—the danger had passed—and simply wobbled out of Clark's office—crutching along his merry way—the tip of the crutch thumping the carpeted floor keeping time as he hummed a few bars of "Rat Face Reggie."

The big man be dumb as a rock, thought Crutch. He also would ask his supervisor for overtime pay. He was, after all, on the job all night long.

Sixty-Eight

Sheldon Clark was pleased with the results of the legacy reduction. Things were right on track. MM had finally eliminated the millstone automotive and truck divisions by simply removing them from the MM family. Some divisions outlived their usefulness and were sold outright. Mega One and Mega Two were the only remaining vehicles assembled in the North America. That would change soon enough. More than 90 percent of their component parts were manufactured offshore.

MM had invested billions of dollars in its overseas operations. Plants in China, Russia, Poland, South Korea, Portugal, Thailand, Africa, Latin America, the mideast and India were doing so well, consideration was being given to moving Detroit's world headquarters to Bombay—but this would not take place for some time—perhaps ten years.

Clark decided to meet with Schmidt and discuss the termination of the ongoing extermination of retirees. The meeting took place at a small motel room in Mohawk, Michigan—a tiny town in Michigan's copper country in the upper peninsula.

Schmidt was not happy to travel the six hundred and fifty miles north from his hideaway in Washington, Michigan, to the nearly unheard town of Mohawk, but in deference to Clark did so.

"Schmidt," said Clark, "it's time to end the legacy. We've accomplished all we set out to do, and have performed admirably. Billions of dollars have been saved. You have exceeded all my expectations. On behalf of Mega Motors, I want to thank you."

Schmidt, for the first time, showed he was not emotionless, and actually produced real tears, but just as quickly as they appeared he wiped them off his cheek with the sleeve of his jacket.

"Mr. Clark," Schmidt softly spoke, "I thank you for the opportunity of helping heal an ailing company. I concur that the job is over. I would ask but one small favor before we part ways."

Clark, deeply touched by Schmidt's sincerity, said, "Anything, Kurt, anything you want."

Schmidt calmly said, "Stop darting your fucking tongue, and don't beg for your life, swine."

Clark looked confused, bewildered, then terrified as Schmidt withdrew his P-38 from its holster. Before Clark could scream, Schmidt killed the CEO of Mega Motors with two well-placed shots to the forehead—each directly above his horrified eyes. Clark was even more homely dead than alive. His tongue remained frozen, sticking out of his cursed thin lips. Schmidt picked up the shell casings and left the motel room. The drive back to Washington, Michigan, was going to be a long, dreadful, eleven-hour trip. He would be exhausted.

Sixty-Nine

News of Sheldon Clark's murder rocked the motor city and business world in general. The New York Stock Exchange suspended operations for one minute before the start of trading Monday morning in a showing of respect for such an important icon of the business world.

The Calumet News reported the murder appeared to have been the work of a professional hit man. No other details were available. People in Michigan's upper peninsula don't spend a lot of time worrying about people down below.

News media did mini reports throughout the country on how great and wonderful Clark had been—how he virtually saved Mega from going under with his remarkable talent and ability to manage the corporation. Nothing derogatory was said, at least in the open. In private, others at the MM building rejoiced.

Behind closed doors at MM's headquarters the walls buzzed with gossip and excitement as to whom the board of directors would choose as Clark's replacement.

Life went on as if nothing happened to people living in the real world. Old Crutch still cleaned offices at the MM building and was working on a new song, called the bullshit blues.

> If Chevys ran on bullshit
> They be no shortage then...

Granted, he needed to refine it a bit, but felt he had a hit in the making. Just might record it himself. Yeah—he figured if cars could run on corn, no reason they wouldn't run on digested corn and hay—or whatever those animals eat. Crutch was definitely a thinker. Hell, he thought, a man have to be smart to keep a step ahead of The Man.

Meanwhile, those remaining active MM employees knew nothing would change for them regardless who the CEO of General Motors was. You couldn't get any further apart than the CEO and a grunt employee.

Ryan and Eleanor were surprised to hear of Clark's murder, but not shocked. Although it may never be proven, they felt strongly Clark had supported Schmidt in the murders of thousands of MM retirees and many of their personal friends.

Schmidt was on the loose—hiding somewhere, they suspected. They would never feel entirely safe as long as he was alive. Their best shot was David, but they hadn't heard from him in several weeks.

Seventy

Schmidt contacted Reich Fuhrer Burger and ordered him to disband the SSS immediately. He directed Burger to give each member ten thousand US dollars and inform his loyal troops to stand in abeyance until further orders. Burger said, "Yes, Mein Fuhrer!" Schmidt could always count on Reich Fuhrer Burger.

Schmidt had some unfinished personal business to attend to. Eleanor, her fiancé, Ryan, and the Jew David had to be exterminated. He knew exactly where Ryan and Eleanor lived, but wasn't positive about David's location. Perhaps he could arrange a situation that would attract David to his American friends.

Ryan awoke at four thirty A.M., showered and kissed Eleanor goodbye. "Leaving for work already?" she asked, barely awake.

"Yep," Ryan said. "The boss let me pick my own hours and I chose six until two thirty. It's a bear getting up, but nice to get out before rush hour. See you a little after three." He kissed her goodbye.

"Bye, sweetie," Eleanor said. "Love you!"

"Bye, babe, love you too," said Ryan.

Shortly after Ryan drove away she thought she heard the backfire of cars, then a few moments later she heard the side door opening. Thinking Ryan had forgotten something, she said, "Did you forget something, honey?" No response. Silence.

Eleanor got out of bed, dressed in one of Ryan's T-shirts and walked out into the kitchen to see Schmidt sitting at her kitchen table drinking a cup of McDonald's coffee. Her legs weakened. She felt sick to her stomach.

Schmidt looked at her up and down and aimed his P-38 at her chest and calmly said, "One word and you are dead. Get dressed. You and I are taking a ride."

He followed her into the bedroom where he watched her dress. He followed her into her bathroom intensely staring and listening as she urinated.

"Don't be shy, Elsie," Schmidt said. "You are perfectly safe—for now."

She dressed as Schmidt curiously watched every detail. He actually selected her clothing, choosing a white blouse over the blue T-shirt Eleanor had removed from her dresser drawer.

She picked up her purse and eased the strap over her shoulder, trembling noticeably.

Schmidt said, "If your handbag feels a little lighter, it's because I removed your toy gun from it," holding the grip of Eleanor's 38 Special between his thumb and forefinger.

"You sick, son of a bitch," said Eleanor.

"Now, now, dear," he grinned, "watch your language. You should be nice to me. If not, I'll have to kill your lover in front of your very blue eyes."

"And, what difference would it possibly make if I'm nice to you?" asked Eleanor.

"None, dear Elsie—none at all. Let's get you into these cuffs and go to my car—now." She put her arms behind her back as Schmidt instructed.

Eleanor knew once she got into Schmidt's vehicle, she had no chance of escaping and little of surviving, but with his gun aimed directly at her, she had little choice. At least she would not die immediately. Once inside the back seat of Schmidt's vehicle, he ordered her to lie down and cuffed her right ankle to an engaged and tightened lap belt. Schmidt blindfolded her eyes with a black cloth and affixed it to the back of her head with velcro strips. She was helpless and mortified.

Two TEE troopers sat lifeless, slumped over their Chevrolet Impala steering wheels—each with 9 mm entrance wounds to the left temple. Schmidt had dressed in his old Detroit Police Department uniform easily able to deceive the troopers who allowed him to innocently approach their unmarked cars. Schmidt thought, it's like shooting stuffed dummies—so simple.

During the twenty-five minute ride from Ryan and Eleanor's house to Schmidt's hideaway in Washington Township, Eleanor's mind raced at warp speed. She had been kidnaped by a monster whose capacity for unspeakable acts far surpassed her ability to imagine. She started to silently say the "Serenity Prayer," then realized she couldn't concentrate long enough to remember the simple, soothing words. She only got as far as "God, grant me" and her mind went blank with fear. Ryan had told her fear was nothing but a lack of faith in God, but this was more than fear—it was sheer nerve-grating terror. The unknown, the unfathomable, relentlessly creeping closer and closer.

She remembered leaving what must have been an expressway as Schmidt's Tahoe made a sharp right turn, stopped, then drove for several minutes on a very smooth road—perhaps asphalt. The vehicle stopped again and then proceeded on what felt and sounded like a gravel road. Pebbles were striking the underbody of the vehicle. An incline was sensed by Eleanor, the vehicle stopped again—then the probable sound of a garage door opening—a short pull ahead, a stop, and then the engine stopped running. She heard the noise of an electric motor closing what must have been a garage door.

Her door opened, and Schmidt removed her ankle cuff from the lap belt and ordered her to slowly scoot out of the back seat and stand on the garage floor. He then led her to an entrance door, which he opened, then into a room that felt and smelled like a kitchen. He then told her to sit down. She sat on what felt like a wooden chair with wooden arms. He unshackled one of her wrists from behind her back and attached the other cuff to the leg of the chair. He then removed her blind fold.

When her eyes adjusted to the blinding light, she observed Schmidt sitting directly across from her, smiling broadly. Both were seated on opposite ends of a rectangular oak dining room table. To her immediate right, and to Schmidt's were empty matching oak chairs.

The dining room was immaculate, well lighted with a beautiful crystal chandelier centered perfectly above the table. One wall featured an exquisite cherry wood china cabinet with mirrored glass highlighting what appeared to be fashionable and very expensive china.

Opposite the china cabinet, on the other wall was an oil painting of an old gray-bearded man saying grace, head bowed in humble gratitude. What an odd painting for a monster to have, Eleanor thought.

"Coffee?" Schmidt asked.

Eleanor said nothing, as Schmidt poured her a steaming cup of rich black coffee in a shiny navy blue mug that was stenciled, "Shit Happens."

When she looked at the slogan on the mug, she couldn't help but smile and wonder what kind of demon could actually have a human sense of humor. Her smile was less than a second in duration, but long enough for Schmidt to observe.

"You think I have no sense of frivolity, Elsie?"

"I think you are a wicked, evil monster, Mr. Schmidt," said Eleanor.

"Of course you do, dear," Schmidt calmly said. "But I am going to show you I am not as evil as you may think."

"And how would you manage that, Mr. Schmidt?"

"First, I insist you call me Kurt. And I will call you Elsie. Humor me please, and this will go much easier on you."

"Why Elsie, Mr. Schmidt, I mean Kurt?" asked a bewildered, frightened Eleanor.

Schmidt thought a moment and concluded there would be no reason she should not know. She would not have the information very long.

"Elsie was my mother's name, Elsie."

"Do I remind you of your mother?" asked Eleanor.

"Not yet," replied Schmidt, grinning maniacally.

"When I last saw my dear mother, she was dead at the behest of my glorious father," Schmidt said, with a morbid glee in his eyes.

"You mean your father killed your mother?" asked Eleanor, fearing his answer.

"She died for the Fuhrer and Germany," said Schmidt who was then standing at rigid attention. He clicked his heels and gave a Nazi salute and screamed a fanatical Heil Hitler!

"Dear God in heaven," moaned Eleanor, finally realizing her fate.

Seventy-One

Ryan was surprised when Eleanor did not answer the telephone when he called her on his lunch break. She hadn't said anything about going anywhere. He called again an hour later with similar results. He started to worry, then assured himself there was no cause to worry. Eleanor was probably out making arrangement for their wedding coming up in less than two weeks.

Thirty minutes before the end of his work day he received a call from Eleanor.

"Ryan?"

"Hi El, I've been trying to reach you. Everything okay?"

Schmidt grabbed the phone from Eleanor's shaking hand and said, "Ryan, this is Kurt Schmidt. I have your fiancée. She is a beautiful little thing. If you want to see her alive again, you and David Wentz will meet us at the Orchards golf course, near the fifth green at six o'clock sharp. If you bring anyone else, or if you come armed, your lover will be unable to attend the wedding."

Ryan was dumfounded. His emotions were stuck between rage and fear.

"Don't hurt her, you bastard," said Ryan.

"You are in no position to give me orders, Conway," said Schmidt.

Ryan continued, "I have no idea where David is."

Schmidt replied, "That's not my problem, is it?"

"For the love of God, Schmidt, please let her go," pleaded Ryan.

Ryan heard the explosion of Schmidt's P-38 along with Eleanor's screams and froze at the sounds.

"Did that get your attention, Ryan?" bellowed Schmidt.

"Be there at six o'clock or the next time my weapon is discharged, your sweet Eleanor's brains will be scattered on the wall," said Schmidt.

"I love you, Ryan," cried Eleanor as Schmidt banged the phone down.

The line went dead.

Ryan quickly removed the slip of paper upon which David had written his cell phone number and made the call.

"Wentz," David answered.

"David, it's Ryan. Schmidt has taken Eleanor and has threatened to kill her unless we meet him at the Orchards at five this afternoon. David, what are we going to do?"

"We are going to meet him," David calmly replied. "I suppose he warned you that we should arrive unarmed."

"Yes, he did," said Ryan, sobbing.

"Ryan, this will not work, unless we are in complete control of our emotions. Try and get a grip. The snake has finally revealed its venomous fangs. Keep the faith and we will be victorious," said David, who fully realized the danger involved, and inwardly felt the same desperation as did Ryan. "I'm in Plymouth now. I'll pick you up at work in twenty minutes. We'll take your Chevy. It's faster than my rental. We'll have plenty of time to get to the Orchards."

Ryan's mind wandered back in time when he and Eleanor first met. He remembered their first date, the softness of their first kiss, and the happiness of her laughter. He couldn't see life without her. Ryan couldn't allow himself to visualize how Schmidt might abuse Eleanor. He wondered how men like Schmidt could be so evil and cruel. Schmidt is not a man, he thought. He is evil personified.

He told his supervisor he might be off work the next few days as something personal had come up. Extremely personal indeed, he thought. A real matter of life and death was more appropriate. Ryan tried to straighten out the items on his desk, but the organization of pens and pencils seemed insignificant. He cut the power to his computer, then realized he was supposed to leave it powered up. He was an emotional wreck. But what about Eleanor? What might she be going through with Schmidt? What if he sexually assaulted her? What if Schmidt killed her? What if, what if, what if? What if I lose my goddamn mind? What if David gets into an accident? Stop it, Ryan!

Orchards Golf Course was relatively free of golfers when David and Ryan arrived at five forty-five. Most of the golfers had finished their rounds and several were in the club house drinking beer and tallying scores, and excuses.

Ryan and David rented a cart for fifteen dollars and rode to the fifth green, a par four of three hundred sixty-five yards. The undulating fairway precluded visual sight of the flag or surface of the bent grass putting surface. The electric cart hummed quietly as the distance closed. They saw nothing on or near the green except the pin, flag, and a few unrepaired ball marks. The flag was at half-mast, indicating the cup was in the middle of the green.

As the two walked carefully on the green, David neared the pin and looked into the cup. He held up the palm of his left hand toward Ryan, motioning for him to stop. Ryan stopped walking as David slowly pulled the pin out of the cup with his right hand. A small box had been taped to the side of the pin. David gently removed the box.

David took a small knife from his pants pocket, removed the pin from the cup and carefully cut the tape away from the top of the box, placing the pin back into the cup. Inside the box was an object wrapped in what appeared to be plain white paper. He unfolded the paper from the object and suddenly dropped them both. An eye, complete with connecting fibrous looking tentacles and a gelatinous substance fell onto the bent grass and rolled several inches before stopping just shy of the cup. "Oh, Jesus Christ," shouted David.

"Please—do—not—tell—me—that's—an—eye!" screamed Ryan.

David was shocked and mortified. He looked at the blood and matter soaked paper that had been wrapped around the eye, and saw a written message. It was from Schmidt.

> Gentlemen,
>
> Keeping an eye out for you! Before you become ill (or are you already?), please note the color of the eye. You will find Eleanor—in one piece—(unless I change my mind) at 313 Mulberry Lane, in Washington Township. Oh, I haven't decided if the piece will be alive.
>
> Regards,
> Kurt Schmidt

"Ryan, Ryan," David said to Ryan who was in a state of shocked denial. "The eye is brown. It's brown, Ryan!"

Ryan had become so upset he was nauseous.

David insisted Ryan sit down on the golf cart and take several deep breaths.

After returning the golf cart to the club house area, David and Ryan started driving to the address Schmidt had written down.

At first, it was difficult for either man to speak. The horror of the incident and the wickedness of Schmidt exceeded what either had expected.

Ryan asked, "David, why would Schmidt give us an address where we could find him? Something isn't kosher."

"He wouldn't," replied David. "He's playing some perverted game. He is crazy as a chicken house rat, Ryan. There is no rhyme or reason to what a madman does. The only constant in his wretched life is the pain and terror he inflicts on others."

"David?"

"Yes, Ryan," answered David.

"What are our chances of saving Eleanor?"

"Do you want an honest answer, Ryan?" David asked.

"Yes, please" said Ryan.

"Slim to none," said David. "But, any chance is worth taking. If Schmidt was not so damn predictably unpredictable."

Seventy-Two

Eleanor thought she might attempt to communicate with Schmidt. She had nothing to lose. Although she would hang onto life as long as possible, inwardly, she knew the end was near, for herself, David and her beloved Ryan.

"Kurt?" asked Eleanor.

"Yes, Elsie," answered Schmidt.

"May I ask you a question?"

"Of course, Elsie."

Schmidt thought, she is going to beg for her life and the lives of Ryan and the Jew David. She will turn into a blubbering slut and I will gut her like a fish.

"Did you love your mother?" Eleanor asked.

The question caught Schmidt completely off guard, and for the first time in years, he was at a complete loss for words.

"Why, uh, well, uh, er, why do you ask?" Schmidt said. "I don't want to talk about it. You…shut…up!"

"Kurt, please tell me," asked Eleanor.

"Why?" bellowed Schmidt. "So you can stall for time? So you can take my mind off the mission?"

"Kurt, I know my time is nearly over. I'm starting to accept that. There are things I must know about you. You view my life is unimportant, but see yours differently. Please tell me about your mother. She and I have the same name. Please, Kurt!"

Schmidt suddenly relaxed, as though a huge weight was lifted from his shoulders. He sat down across the dining room table from Eleanor and talked.

"First, I do not view your life as insignificant, as you will discover soon enough," Schmidt said.

"My mother was the most beautiful woman in Germany—no—in the world. She cared for me—loved and nurtured me. She told me bedtime stories and calmed my fears when the war started to go badly against Germany. She was a perfect—well—almost a perfect mother.

"She held me tightly during allied raids and comforted me when our lights were out, and as the bombs shook our home. She told me she loved me more than life itself, and would gladly give her life to save mine.

"She told me Hitler had done a terrible injustice to Germany. That he was a madman and a fool. She said he was a sadist and had millions of innocent Jews put to death for no cause.

"Then she said my father had been disillusioned by Hitler. Papa was basically a good man, but the things he was doing—killing Czechs, Poles, Russians and Jews were evil, just like Hitler.

"Then she said, Kurt, my little boy, I will always love you, no matter what happens."

Eleanor, feeling a pang of pity for this demented man said, "Oh, Kurt, what did you do then?"

Schmidt said, "I told my Papa what she said. Papa said, your mother must be sacrificed for uttering blasphemous nonsense about the Fuhrer and Germany. He told me to get his stiletto and stab mother in the heart when she was sleeping.

"I did what Papa told me. I always did. That night, after my mother fell asleep, I went into her bedroom and lay down beside her. She awoke for a moment, put her arms around me, told me how much she loved me, and fell back to sleep. After I knew she was asleep, I plunged the stiletto into her chest with all my might, and she awoke in exquisite pain, screaming. She stared at me, refusing to believe what I'd done. Moments later, as she lay dying, she softly said, 'Kurt, I forgive and love you.'"

"God, Kurt, what did you do then?" asked Eleanor.

"That, Elsie, I will not say," said Schmidt.

"Please, Kurt. Unburden yourself of the misery," pleaded Eleanor. "You've gone this far. Tell me the rest."

"Very well, if you insist," said Schmidt.

"After my mother died, I had sex with her corpse."

"Oh no, no, NO!" Eleanor screamed hysterically.

"May God forgive you, because I cannot," said Eleanor. "No man or woman could forgive you."

"Neither will God, Elsie. Neither will God."

"Now, my dear Elsie, it's time to remove your clothes. Mother was naked when she died," said Schmidt.

Schmidt forced a nude Eleanor upstairs, into his bedroom, where he ordered her to lie down on the bed. He then removed a nylon cord and affixed her wrists to the head posts of the queen size bed, and her ankles to the knobbed footboard. She lay naked, helpless, staring at the textured green ceiling. She started saying the Lord's Prayer—over and over again.

Schmidt left the bedroom for several minutes and returned attired in his father's black SS officer's uniform, a highly polished black steel helmet, spit-shined jack boots, and a belted, holstered P-38. Death's head insignias adorned his helmet as did the feared SS lightning stripes. He proudly wore his father's German Cross around his neck. Kurt Schmidt was dressed to kill. His arrogance formed an invisible uniform around his large sinister frame.

Seventy-Three

As David and Ryan approached the Mulberry Street address, Michigan's pale sun was beginning the dip into the western horizon. Both men had made sure their weapons were cleaned and loaded.

David was surprised to see two garage coach lights turned on. Several inside lights glowed brightly as well. What the hell? David wondered.

"Listen, Ryan, you stay in the car and I'll sneak up to the front door." David had parked the Impala in front of the neighbor's house.

"No way in hell I'm going to stay here," said Ryan.

"Then stay behind me, Ryan. That's an order," David sternly said.

Both had their weapons drawn when David tried the front door lock. It opened easily. He doubted anyone was home.

Each looked around the living room, and saw nothing. Just a well-decorated home—nothing more. They walked into the great room, then the kitchen and dining area. No sign of life. Ryan motioned to David the door leading to the basement. David started to open the white enameled basement door and they both heard a squeaking sound. The squeak sounded like the noise of a bed spring. They listened carefully. There it was again. It was coming from upstairs.

They quietly ascended the fourteen carpeted steps to where the squeaking noise originated. David, still in the lead, stopped at the top of the steps and pointed with his gun barrel toward a yellow glow shining under a closed green-paneled door.

They tensed upon hearing the distinctive sound of a semiautomatic handgun being racked for action. Could it be Schmidt?

With hand signals and head movements, David motioned for Ryan to stand directly behind him. After walking to the door, David would suddenly open it, fall onto the floor and assume a prone shooting position. Ryan would be the back-up and shoot to kill should Schmidt or any of his cronies be in the room.

Schmidt, speaking boldly, clearly and with authority, said, "Come in, gentlemen, the door is open. Please come in"

As David slowly opened the door, he immediately lowered his gun to his side. Ryan did the same.

Schmidt was standing adjacent to the bed—his Walther P-38 inches away from Eleanor's left temple. She was completely naked, bound to the bed with nylon rope. Duct tape sealed her mouth, but her frightened blue eyes revealed horror, shame and a certain awareness of impending death.

Schmidt stood perfectly rigid, showing no signs of nervousness whatsoever. His right trigger finger pulsed slightly on the trigger of the P-38.

"Yes," Schmidt said. "I could have killed Elsie and escaped quite easily. You dullards are no match for me. However, I decided to allow you the privilege of watching me kill Elsie—I'm sorry, you still think of her as Eleanor.

"First, however, I insist that you, Jew David and Ryan, drop your weapons to the floor. Now!" said Schmidt.

Schmidt reached over Eleanor's head then tore the duct tape from her mouth.

She winced, but said nothing. Her eyes were fixed on Ryan.

"There's nothing like the healthy scream of a young woman in the final seconds of her life to liven the scene, wouldn't you agree?" Schmidt said.

As David and Ryan reluctantly let their guns fall to the mauve carpeted floor, Schmidt fired, hitting David squarely in the chest. David slowly slumped to his knees, then fell, face first to the floor.

Schmidt suddenly brought his gun around to Eleanor's head but in an instant before her life ended, she uttered, "Elsie loves you, Kurt."

Kurt Schmidt hesitated just long enough for Ryan to retrieve his .357 magnum and squeeze off one round. The hydro-shok bullet tore into Schmidt's forehead killing him instantly. His body fell directly across Eleanor's, as she screamed in terror and revulsion.

Ryan quickly pulled Schmidt off Eleanor, pushed his lifeless remains onto the floor and untied her. He found a blanket nearby and draped it across her shaking, naked body. She stood up, although weak and badly unnerved, and hugged her hero, Ryan.

"I love you, Ryan. I knew you would be here for me."

"I love you too, El."

"Poor David," she motioned to his lifeless body. "The poor, brave man."

David groaned, then slowly moved, finally sat up and muttered, "Thank God for good friends and Kevlar."

"Thank God. You are safe, David!" Ryan said. "Thank God."

"Amen," cried Eleanor.

Arising slowly, in obvious pain, David said, "Let's shut off the lights and get the hell out of here."

David, Ryan, and Eleanor left Schmidt's Washington Township home, headed south in Ryan's Chevy Impala. David sat in the back seat of the Chevy. As they neared Lakeside Shopping Center, Eleanor suddenly looked at her left hand.

"Oh my God, Ryan, I just remembered. Schmidt removed my engagement ring and put it in his watch-pocket."

"Do you want to go back and get it?" asked Ryan.

"As much as I hate going anywhere near him or his house, I must have the ring," said Eleanor. "Would you mind terribly if we went back?"

As the three pulled into Schmidt's driveway, they were relieved to see the lights still off. David was concerned one of Schmidt's neighbors might have called the local police, but apparently this had not been the case.

"I'll go in and get it," said David.

"I'll go with you," suggested Ryan.

"And leave me alone in the car? No way," Eleanor said.

The three entered the darkened house and found the light switch for the stairway. Ryan and Eleanor, holding hands, followed David up the flight of stairs and entered the bedroom slowly. The room smelled of cordite and fresh blood.

David hesitated a moment, before he said, "Damn it!"

"What the hell?" Ryan said.

Nearly in unison, they all said, "He's not here!"

"Son of a bitch," said Ryan.

They scurried out of the house then drove south to Warren.

Few words were spoken. Their thoughts were private and frightening.

Seventy-Four

Eleanor and Ryan were married in less than two weeks in an informal ceremony. David was the best man, and exceedingly proud to have been asked.

Ryan asked David why he did not wear his yarmulka to the wedding. David told him it was only worn to cover bald spots on Jewish men. They had a good laugh when Ryan finally realized David was joking.

Before the newly wedded couple left for their Traverse City honeymoon, Ryan shook David's hand and gave him a manly hug.

"You are a good man, for a spook," Ryan jokingly said.

"Quiet, you'll blow my cover," David quipped.

Eleanor decided David was worthy of a hug and a kiss. And he certainly was.

After the kiss, David told Ryan, "You are a very lucky man, indeed."

Ryan smiled at David, then Eleanor and said, "I am the luckiest man alive."

David told Ryan and Eleanor they had both been appointed honorary sayanim (Mossad helpers) and invited them to visit him in Tel Aviv. They said they would—but of course they wouldn't.

Ryan and Eleanor told David he would always be welcome to stay with them whenever he returned to Michigan. He appreciated the offer and said he would, but he probably wouldn't.

They parted ways, the best of friends, and would continue to be so for the foreseeable future, and perhaps beyond.

Seventy-Five

Mega Motors Corporation still made great cars and trucks—unfortunately, few were assembled in America. This was of course the plan all along—to downsize by outsourcing using the economic global necessity scam as the primary reason. Individuals with cork for brains knew the real reason was money, greed, and power.

The only MM vehicles assembled in America were the Mega 1and Mega 2. Plans to combine both, to be named the Mega 3, were to be announced soon.

The Mega 3 featured a combined front, rear-wheel, or all-wheel drive option at the flick of a button. The transmission was a refined turbo-glide with overdrive that engaged flawlessly at exactly forty miles per hour. Each vehicle was equipped with every available option included in the sticker price. Windshield wipers had been replaced with a blower and vacuum system that silently removed all water that touched the windshield by efficiently blowing droplets of rain, sleet or snow with a jet of warm air from the base of the windshield to louvers located at the top of the windshield, then directed to the ground below. The Mega 3 had dozens of creature comforts, including an altimeter and barometer.

The newly designed piston engine burned gasoline, diesel, ethanol, peanut oil, sunflower, corn, or virtually any combination of combustible liquid. The wheel, disc and tire were one unique assembly made of space-age polymers. The engine block itself was plastic, as were its moving components.

Although the piston multi-fuel supercharged engine was by far the most popular, electric, battery-powered mini-megas were available for earth worshipers who felt any explosive liquid was harmful to the earth's atmosphere.

Air bags were replaced with safety seats that protected the driver and passenger(s) upon any impact more than fifteen miles per hour. Passengers and drivers remained unharmed in collisions up to eighty miles per hour. The safety seat system made seat belts, harnesses and air bags obsolete. The miraculous safety seats were completely restorable and reusable immediately after deployment. Traffic fatalities were virtually eliminated using this advanced American technology. Finally, the American driver could drive without fear of killing or being killed on our highways without being belted and harnessed like a horse pulling a buggy.

Vehicle warranty was extended from a mere hundred thousand to one million miles, or life of the owner. The warranty was, of course, non transferrable. MM banked on owners tiring of the vehicle and buying another before warranty issues arose.

MM's upper management remained as smug and arrogant as they had been during the Clark era. Such people simply do not learn. Few knew that pensions would soon be a thing of the past. Health care would be available only if employees paid the lion's share of the premium. Hourly employees' wages would be reduced by 50 percent over the next several contracts. Cost of living allowance for retirees and active union employees would be eliminated. If the union did not give in the company demands, the company would simply close shop and move overseas.

For a few years, MM gave the UAW complete control over managing the health care system of hourly retirees at the expense of hourly employees, and retirees. When the union realized it was an unmanageable situation, they attempted to transfer the health care program back to the corporation, who simply refused the task resulting in zero health care benefits, unless the union was willing to make additional wage concessions.

Still, MM employees and retirees remained loyal and 85 percent of them continued to purchase vehicles manufactured by MM who anticipated US employment of ten thousand hourly, along with two thousand salaried employees. Of the two thousand salaried employees, five hundred were junior and senior executives.

With the legacy solution having been nearly fully implemented, letters were mailed to all active and retired employees complaining of ever-increasing benefit, labor and material costs, and the need to take action to become more cost competitive. The nature of the action would be disclosed at a later date. The letter did state, however, that action was inevitable.

Life insurance, which had been provided by MM, free of charge, was a thing of the past—cancelled for all active and retired individuals. Dental, vision and hearing insurance was no longer provided. Virtually any benefit not mandated by federal or state law was eliminated.

Legacy costs now included projected/anticipated costs not yet incurred. Costs where no reserve or debit funds had been established fell within the new definition of legacy. Clark's bold solution to legacy cost control had opened a Pandora's box of opportunity for bean counters and other cost control freaks across the corporation, and eventually across corporate America.

These estimated ghost liabilities were calculated by overpaid analysts, presented to their respective supervisors, given approval and forwarded to section junior executives for discussion, and implementation.

Each $100,000.00 in ghost or phantom cost resulted in the elimination of one active hourly or salary employee. Whether accomplished by actual displacement or retirement was insignificant. What was paramount was the elimination of employees in adherence with this down sourcing formula.

Ryan wondered who would buy the millions of vehicles now being mass-produced in foreign countries, and just as quickly, dismissed the thought. What should have been done to avoid the loss of the American automobile industry should have been done decades ago by corporations who loved America more than personal power. But did corporate executives have a heart? Of course not, he concluded.

Seventy-Six

Sometimes, when the nights were still and serene, tearful thoughts of lost friends crossed Ryan and Eleanor's minds. It was nearly impossible to avoid dwelling on the past. In time, happier thoughts would replace the ones fraught with sadness and misery, but when they allowed themselves a mere glimpse of past evil, the nightmares returned in vivid gory detail.

Occasionally, when storms rich with cold rain, thunder and lightning marched over southeast lower Michigan, sinister thoughts surfaced. Demon memories were the most difficult to elude. With each brilliant, crooked flash of lightning, and booming break of thunder, there stood an even chance of viewing a monster viewing you with extreme malice.

With the likes of Schmidt and Clark gone forever, life would most certainly be a more wondrous and beautiful experience. The horrors of the past were in the past—gone forever. Just concentrate on the present, they thought.

One cold, gray, typically Michigan January afternoon, Eleanor received a registered letter from an unknown sender. Who on earth, she wondered?

She opened the envelope, curious as to who would have sent it. The contents read:

> Ms. Elsie Conway:
>
> I will return your ring.
>
> Reich Fuhrer Hans Burger

Eleanor, in a state of bewildered despair and shock, dropped the letter and screamed, "Ryan!"

Seventy-Seven

Reich Fuhrer Hans Burger did not aspire to become Fuhrer. As Reich Fuhrer of the SSS, he had no superiors. He was answerable only to his conscience, and to the duty transferred to him upon the death of Kurt Schmidt, the last true and absolute Fuhrer since Adolph Hitler.

His sworn duty was twofold. First he would personally kill Elsie (Eleanor) Conway, then her husband, Ryan, and finally Jew David—if he was in country. Of course, these killings were mere appetizers—hardly a challenge.

Burger's mission was to destroy the morale of the American people. The Reich Fuhrer thought, thanks to the ineptitude of the blundering republican and democrat political parties, his task had been made much easier. Still, he knew Yankees were a resilient lot and much work remained.

First things first, he thought. He composed a poem for Elsie. It would be delivered to her in tomorrow's mail.

Reflections of you
Sweet subtle view
Not the least faded by time
I'll soon see you dead
Yes, off with your head
Elsie, dear Elsie, you swine.
–H.B.

Hans, Hans, he thought—*you should have been a poet.* He folded the work neatly and placed it in a self-sticking envelope addressed to Ms. E. Conway. Latex gloves were such a clever German invention.

Seventy-Eight

"Ryan, are you going to your meeting tonight?" asked Eleanor.

"*My* meeting, dear?"

"You know what I mean, Mr. Smarty Pants," said Eleanor.

"Yes, El, I'm going. You want to come along? It's an open meeting," said Ryan.

"I think I'll stay home, if you don't mind. I have a slight headache."

"Take a couple of aspirin," said Ryan.

"I probably will, Doctor Conway."

"Great. Well, I'm going to go in a little early. My turn to make coffee, again," said Ryan.

"You seem to have problems getting dependable coffee makers, Ryan."

"If you only knew," muttered Ryan.

"What?" said Elsie.

"Nothing, El. See you a little after nine," Ryan said.

"Bye, Ryan."

Eleanor watched television while Ryan was at the meeting. She reflected on how much he had changed. He was the perfect husband so long as he stayed sober. Her ultimatum was challenging. She told him that he had a choice—alcohol or her, but not both. She wondered if she could leave him—really leave him, should he start drinking. She prayed she wouldn't have to make that decision. How was she to understand the disease concept of alcoholism when it was not fully understood by anyone?

A single day at a time for Ryan and her—that's what it was all about. She would never understand what drove alcoholics to participate in something so destructive—something that would surely destroy them physically, emotionally and spiritually. As long as Ryan stayed sober, life was wonderful.

She would tell him after the meeting. It would be a terrific surprise. They had tried for a year. Ryan had made an appointment with a doctor who, Ryan supposed, would put him in a closed room with a dirty magazine and small cup and wait for him to produce a sample of his seed for microscopic examination. No doubt, he thought, they would find him sterile as a stick. God, he was in for a surprise, Eleanor thought.

"Did you have a good meeting, honey?" asked Eleanor.

"It was great," replied Ryan.

"Sit down, Ryan."

"What's wrong?"

"You'll need to cancel your appointment with Doctor Schwartz," said a somber Eleanor.

"Why? Don't you remember how long it took to get in to see that guy?" said a curious and mystified Ryan.

"You don't get it, do you?"

"Get what?" said Ryan. "You don't mean that...you...are...pregnant?"

"Well, you could still go whack off in a cup if you wanted to, but, yes, I'm pregnant. A forty-year-old pregnant broad. Isn't that something?"

"Hell, the daddy isn't exactly a spring chicken. I'm older than you," said a jubilant Ryan.

It was one of the happiest moments of their lives. They hugged and kissed, went to bed—hugged, kissed, and gently made love for the next hour.

Seventy-Nine

Ryan awoke at five o'clock the next morning. He showered and shaved, dressed and kissed Eleanor goodbye. He filled his stainless steel coffee mug, snapped the lid shut and whistled a cheery tune as he walked out the front door on his way to work at the MM benefits office. His coffee mug had been a gift from MM after once purchasing an MM SUV. The cup was emblazoned, "MMTrucks."

His Impala SS started instantly, and he inserted a Janis Joplin CD in the player and happily drove to work. Life was good. He had not picked up a drink in nearly eighteen months, and had no desire to today.

Eleanor slept in until nearly eight o'clock, got up and poured a cup of very strong black coffee. She sat down at the kitchen table with the morning edition of the Detroit Free Press thinking about the baby to be between headlines. She was in her first trimester and as yet did not know the sex of the baby to be. She had no preference, and knew Ryan felt the same. Then she thought—*Gosh. I'll be fifty-eight when the kid gets out of high school.* I *may be wearing diapers!*

Bob, the friendly mail carrier, delivered the mail early. He usually showed up at one P.M., but was even earlier today—it was only twelve-thirty. Bob was the nicest, most efficient mailman she had ever known. His government-gray uniform neatly pressed, and he was very well groomed. He was a proud American, and chose to be that rather than a proud African-American. The days of suburban racism were slowly changing. Both black and white started to realize they were much more alike than not.

Bob and his wife lived in a well-maintained home in Detroit, but had purchased a home in once lily-white Warren. They looked forward to retirement in Warren, and would rent their Detroit home for added income.

"Good morning, Bob," said Eleanor, as she met him on the front porch.

"Hello, Mrs. Conway," responded Bob, cheerfully. "Not much for you today. Just an electric bill and one letter."

As she took the mail from Bob, she said, "Thanks, Bob, have a good day."

"Thank you, Mrs. Conway—you too," said Bob as he pushed his three-wheeled mail cart down the drive.

Eleanor watched as Bob walked briskly to his cart. She thought, *I never saw anyone walk as swiftly as Bob.*

Wow, she thought, the electric bill (once called the Edison bill) is getting higher each month. By the time she had walked into the living she had noticed there was no return address on the envelope addressed to her. She sat down on the living room couch, opened the envelope and slowly read the horrible poem sent by Hans Burger. She dropped the letter to the floor, covered both eyes with the damp palms of her trembling hands and wept.

Ryan stopped at the local florist on his way home from work to purchase one dozen yellow, long-stemmed roses he had ordered earlier from Jerry's Florist. Eleanor loved flowers, but the yellow rose was her favorite.

As Ryan proudly walked into the living room, concealing the rose bouquet behind his back, he immediately saw Eleanor, sitting on the couch, still wearing her red silk pajamas. Her eyes were swollen and red from crying. The flowers became secondary. He hurriedly placed them on their side on the medium-oak coffee table, sat down, and lovingly embraced her.

"What's wrong, El? Talk to me."

"That dirty son of a bitch. The sorry evil, rotten bastard," Eleanor cursed.

"Who are you talking about, El?"

Eleanor handed Ryan the letter/poem from Burger. It wasn't a threat. It was a promise—a nightmarish death sentence.

Ryan immediately called the local police department, stating his wife had received a death threat in the mail. The officer told Ryan the police could not do much in that the letter had not been signed.

Ryan attempted to convince the officer that he and Eleanor knew who sent the letter, but, again, the officer courteously stated there was nothing to be done until a more specific and credible threat occurred. Ryan was advised to contact the offices of the FBI in Detroit and was given their toll-free number.

He placed a call to the FBI and spoke with an agent Holland. Agent Holland was aware of Hans Burger, and made an appointment to see the Eleanor and Ryan. Agent Holland asked Ryan to not handle the letter or envelope, as he would bring this evidence back to his office where it would be checked for prints, etc.

Ryan felt nothing would be done to protect Eleanor until Burger attempted to carry out his threat—and then what?

Finally, Ryan decided to call his friend David Wentz in Tel Aviv, Israel. He realized with a seven-hour time differential, getting through to David would be highly unlikely. It was nearly midnight in Israel. After overcoming several dialing obstacles, Ryan was eventually connected to David's voice mail.

He left the following message. "David, it's Ryan Conway. Burger threatened Eleanor's life. I've contacted the local authorities and the FBI. They say there isn't much they can or will do right now. We need your help, David. Please call."

Eighty

David checked his voice mail the following morning. After listening to Ryan's message he was livid. He had hoped the lunatic Burger would have gone into hiding. He doubted if the Mossad Director would authorize another trip to America, but he would certainly ask.

The more David thought about Burger's threat, the more furious he became. He wondered, will the Nazi bastards ever stop? He answered his own question. No, of course not.